Movie Star
Cowboy

Cowboy Hero, Book 8

Barbara McMahon

Movie Star Cowboy
Copyright © 2016 Barbara McMahon
All Rights Reserved

One

Trouble.

The moment she saw the powerful motorcycle roar past the compound and continue on the road that led directly to Windhaven Ranch, she knew it only spelled trouble. The big black machine kicked up the dust as it thundered closer, shattering the tranquility of the summer morning. The driver wore black, his face and hair hidden behind the black helmet which reflected the sun like a halo.

Kelsey knew it was no angel coming–only trouble with a capital T.

She took a deep breath, held it a couple of seconds, then let it go with a whoosh, trying to relax nerves that felt stretched to the breaking point. Butterflies danced in her stomach and uncertainty filled her. Her heart beat faster in a mix of excitement, anticipation and dread.

Then anger surged. Blessed, calming anger. She refused to let the inevitable encounter upset her. She was a survivor. Hadn't the last four years proved that? She'd handle him as she handled everything these days—confidently and competently and on her own terms.

Kelsey tracked his progress from the upstairs

window, watched as he skillfully negotiated the sharp turn into the gravel driveway, barely slowing the machine, its roar powerful in the afternoon stillness. It almost seemed for a second that he'd tip over, but another burst of speed sent pulsating waves of energy to the wheels and he completed the turn with only a cloud of dust to mark his passage.

Kelsey felt the raw power of the big motorcycle exploited by the rider. When he pulled up before the old wooden house, he stopped and cut the engine. The sudden silence was startling after the throaty growl of the cycle. For a long moment, the man sat astride the bike gazing at the shabby, neglected house, the sagging porch, the weeds in the front yard.

He threw his leg over and stood, reaching up to pull the helmet off and run his fingers through his dark hair.

She remembered the gesture so well and wished she didn't.

He looked around again, back from where he'd come, to the barn and buildings in the distance, across to the fenced fields and beyond to the faint line of hills at the far horizon. She watched him assess the place.

For a moment Kelsey thought he resembled a pirate— bold, bad and brazen. She knew even before he turned what he'd look like. The deep tan was a surprise, but nothing else had changed. His broad shoulders tapered to narrow hips. His long legs were muscular and firmly planted on the Texas soil. His eyes would be black as midnight. And his smile would melt the hardest stone.

She sighed as she turned from the window. Better get it over with. She hoped and even prayed that when he received her letter he'd respond by mail. She didn't want to see him again.

Little had ever gone the way she wanted when around Jared, so why did she think it'd start now?

The squeak of the screen door as she pushed it open a moment later drew his attention. He turned swiftly and stared into Kelsey's calm face. She'd hold that impassive look until dark if needed. And never let him suspect the effort it cost her.

She remained silent, letting the door bang shut behind her as she studied her once beloved cousin Jared. Fourth cousin, actually, but as kids she'd claimed that relationship. Had reveled in it.

Times sure changed.

"Hello, love," he said, his smile a trifle uncertain, a certain vulnerability in his gaze.

He was good, she had to give him that. But that was what he did. And he'd always been good at it. No one became a world-famous movie star by lousy acting. Jared had never been vulnerable in his life. What was he trying to accomplish by this act now?

Why had he come?

"We both know that's the wrong thing to call me, Jared. What are you doing here?" Her voice was neutral, emotionless. Was it too much to hope he'd tell her, get back on the bike and take off?

Of course it was.

The smile left his face and his expression became withdrawn. His eyes insolently roamed over her. Kelsey's anger rocketed up a notch. She wished she'd worn a sweatshirt and baggy jeans, but it was too hot for that. July was the height of the summer. And she hadn't known he was coming.

He quickly mounted the three steps to the porch, the wood groaning beneath his weight.

"Is this place even safe?"

He frowned, testing the springy boards beneath his feet.

"It needs some work. Structurally, it's sound. I wrote you."

Afraid he'd come closer, afraid he'd trap her between his body and the house, she moved to the flimsy railing that encircled the left side of the porch. She leaned against it, hoping it wouldn't give way beneath her while she kept a wary eye on him.

"I stopped by the real estate office in town, to ask them about selling that place. They're coming out to look at it this week to give us an estimate on a sale price," he said without warning.

"What? You had no right to do that!"

His calm announcement brought her back upright and she took a step closer. That was so like him. Charge ahead and not consult anyone.

"This place is half mine and I'm not planning to sell. I wrote you to offer to buy out your half!"

Anger spilled out. Her detached air vanished. How dared he talk about putting the ranch up for sale without consulting her?

Could he even do that legally?

"With what? This place had to be worth something and I doubt you have the money to come up with half."

His expression remained aloof.

"Or have you come into money I don't know about?"

"I may need a little time," she said. They both knew she didn't have enough money on hand to buy half a Texas ranch.

"Time's one thing I don't have. If you can't buy me out, then we sell."

He stated it as if it were settled.

For one startling moment anger blazed through Kelsey. She refused to be dictated to by this arrogant man. Never again would she allow herself to be used to to further someone else' goal.

She wanted this ranch and she'd fight for it. He didn't know her any more, if he ever had.

She wasn't the shy, malleable young girl he'd once known. She'd changed dramatically–and in part due to him.

She took a breath and moved back to the railing, turning her back on him, gazing out over the land towards the distant rim of hills. Her heart pounded with anger. Blood rushed through her veins, echoing in her ears. She wouldn't let him upset her. She was stronger now, much stronger than four years ago.

And she'd keep this property! It was her inheritance and she had plans.

"You can't sell without my consent and that you'll never have. If you want to see if we can work something out, for me to buy you out, fine. If not, you're stuck as half owner. I'm not selling."

She fisted her hands. She should have figured he'd be a problem.

"Oh, so the kitten has claws," he murmured, stepping

closer, the old porch groaning beneath his weight.

The strong feeling of longing that rose in him surprised him, threatening to overwhelm him by merely gazing at Kelsey. He wanted to touch her. Hug her. Kiss her.

"Go away. I won't be charmed by you."

She refused to meet his eyes, afraid she might be swayed by his charm after all. Still annoyed by her involuntary reactions to him.

His laughter surprised her and she turned in surprise.

"Oh, love, that's priceless."

His grin was genuine.

He laughed and the change in his expression caused Kelsey to glimpse the young man she'd known years—the daring and darling distant cousin from the other side of the state whom she'd once worshiped.

Her heart rate increased and she looked away. The past was gone. She was much wiser now. She refused to let herself get involved again. He was nothing but trouble and she wanted him out of her life for good.

"Be serious, Kelsey, what do you want with this old ranch? If this house is anything to go by, Uncle Henry let the entire place fall into ruin. It'll fetch something on the market, of course, land is always valuable. But my guess is not much. Be realistic—neither one of us has the slightest idea about running a cattle ranch. What are you trying to prove?"

"I'm not trying to prove anything," she said.

She'd already proved all she needed to. To herself and her family. She didn't need to explain anything to Jared Martin.

"Then tell me, why are you so adamant to keep Windhaven?"

She debated not telling him, but he'd find out, and sooner rather than later.

Still she hesitated. She hated to reveal anything about herself–especially her fragile dreams. She wanted as much distance between the two of them as possible. She wanted her life closed to him.

When she glanced at him over her shoulder, she found his dark eyes staring steadily back at her. He wouldn't leave until he had his explanation. He'd always been stubborn as a mule.

Pushing away the memories that flooded, she tilted her chin as she faced him.

"I want to move my business here. There's room to expand and I can use the space."

"What business?"

He seemed genuinely puzzled. Hadn't he heard she had her own business?

That was interesting.

She was sure someone in the family kept him apprised of what she was doing. Was it possible that he'd heard nothing about her in the last four years?

Jared studied her for a long moment. The family was on her side. They obviously felt the need to shelter her from knowing what she was doing. That hurt.

Shifting slightly against the railing, Kelsey turned to face him, steeling her heart against the draw it felt towards Jared.

"Grandma Mary's Cookies," she said shortly.

When her marriage ended so abruptly, she'd been too

proud to return to her parents' home. They'd been against her marriage from the beginning. She'd ignored them and followed her heart. A mistake she'd regretted.

Because pride prevented her from returning home, she'd been desperate for some way to earn a living. Not trained for anything, she'd quickly found baking a lucrative endeavor making the delicious cookie desserts from the recipes she'd been given by her grandmother.

She began in her own small flat in Dallas. Before long she'd cornered the market there for specialty shops.

Two years ago she'd expanded throughout Texas. Now she supplied Grandma Mary's Cookies to small grocery stores and specialty shops throughout the state.

Windhaven Ranch offered an opportunity to expand, enabling her to move into other markets, perhaps even go national.

Kelsey was determined to succeed in this, as she hadn't in their marriage. She wouldn't let the past or Jared stand in her way. She was proud of what she'd accomplished. And she had plans to accomplish even more.

"Cookies?" Jared asked, trying to remember where he'd heard the name.

Were they the cookies his mother sometimes sent to him when he was on location? The ones in the fancy box with the old-fashioned bonnet on them?

"Yes."

She wasn't talking to him any more than she needed. She suspected he'd scoff at any ideas she had.

"You want this ranch to make cookies?" He couldn't believe it. "Kelsey, are you nuts? This place is more than a giant kitchen, for heaven's sake. It was once one of the largest cattle ranches in the area."

"I know. I planned to keep the cowboys on. Let them take care of the cattle. Look at this setting. It's pastoral and gorgeous. Once fixed up, it'll be the perfect background for Grandma Mary's Cookies. I'll fix up the house and open a tearoom so tourists can come to see Grandma's house."

Her tone was half proud, half defiant. She'd thought it through for months, poured over spreadsheets with financial calculations. Trying to envision every scenario ever since she heard their uncle had left them the property.

"Tourists?" He leaned against the railing, ignoring the way it moved beneath his weight, his eyes never left hers. "Is the sun too hot for you?"

"We're only an hour or so from Dallas. People on vacation would love to see a working ranch. I want to offer the ambiance of a country farmhouse, something people would expect when buying cookies from Grandma."

"We're more than an hour from Dallas, closer to two. Not an easy jaunt for someone looking for a tearoom. This place is falling down. No one would buy anything from this dump. Uncle Henry was in his late nineties when he died. He obviously did nothing around here in the last twenty years. It'll cost a fortune to fix up the house enough to make it habitable, not to mention installing a commercial kitchen up to code. For what, a few cookies? Sell it, Kelsey, and use the money you get to buy a tearoom in Dallas."

"Nope." She shook her head firmly. "I'm not selling! It was Uncle Henry's and his father's before that. This ranch has been in my family for generations and he left it to me. I'm going to keep it and use it for my business."

"He was a relative of mine, too, cousin. But I don't have those idealistic romantic notions about keeping something solely because it's been in the family for years."

"We all are aware of how you treat family," she bit out, standing away from the railing, anger threatening to engulf her.

Why couldn't she have gotten over him years ago?

"Family means nothing to you. Go do your thing in the movie business and leave the rest of us real people to do real work. Name your price for your half and I'll see what I can do to meet it."

She stalked across the porch and threw open the screen, letting it slam behind her with a most satisfactory smack.

She'd only taken a few steps down the hall towards the kitchen when she heard his heavy tread behind her. The screen door slammed again just as his hand caught her arm and spun her around, his fingers tight on the bare skin of her upper arm.

Startled, she gazed up into his blazing eyes. Acting or not, the performance was intimidating. Had she pushed too far?

She licked her lips and stood as tall as her five feet four inches would allow. Jared still towered over her at six feet. His dark hair was tousled from his helmet, his dark eyes bore down into hers.

She refused to be intimidated.

"Why have you come? We could have handled this all by mail or over the phone. Things couldn't have changed that much in four years. Go away, Jared. Go back to LA."

"I can't do that, Kelsey," he said, relaxing his hold on her, his fingers now caressing the soft skin of her arm, sending shivers of longing and delight coursing through her. His voice softened, his face gradually lost the anger.

"I'm not ready to leave Texas."

"Why did you come? Just to sell the ranch? I told you in my letter I'd buy out your half."

"I'd have handled that by mail, if that's what I wanted."

He studied her for a long moment, his eyes narrowed, his dark irises almost the same color as his pupils.

Kelsey stared back, thoughts mixed up and churning in her head. Flashbacks of their time together as kids, the hero-worship she'd had for her exciting cousin on his occasional visits to her parents' place.

"I've come home to claim my wife," he said at last.

Her face changed, the memories of her childhood vanishing in an instant as the pain of betrayal swamped her again.

She yanked her arm from his gentle fingers and stepped back. "Go away. Your joke's in poor taste!"

Running as though the devil himself were behind her, Kelsey dashed through the kitchen, out of the back door and across the fields towards the small walnut orchard Uncle Henry had been so proud of.

She wanted as much distance between herself and Jared as she could get.

It'd been so much easier when he was in different

countries filming. Blast it, why had he chosen now to return? Why couldn't he have just stayed in Los Angeles or England or wherever he'd most recently been and accepted her offer to buy out his half?

Why was he stirring up old emotions best left dormant?

He was trouble, plain and simple.

Kelsey checked to make sure she wasn't being followed then slowed her pace.

The day was hot, the air sultry. She found a tree with a low branch and swung up into it, settling against the trunk, breathing hard.

Now what? Would he let her buy his share? Pressure her to sell? What?

And how long did she have before she said or did something she'd regret?

It was harder than she'd expected to face him, to talk to him. She wished fervently that he'd leave. She hoped he'd be gone by the time she returned to the house. Wishful thinking, she knew.

If he wanted something, he pushed for it and never gave up. He'd been so stubborn as long as she'd known him. He hadn't changed.

That was one trait that led to his successful career as an actor, first in made for television films, then on the big screen. He was a huge success in Hollywood, something that came rarely. And he'd achieved it by determination and perseverance and old-fashioned stubbornness.

And his talent.

He was good, she had to give him that.

Kelsey remembered some of his earlier adventure

films, with a romantic subplot. Lots of action and fast-paced plots—and he always got the girl.

She hadn't seen any of the more recent ones he'd starred in.

Throughout the afternoon she listened for the sound of the motorcycle which would alert her he was leaving. It never came.

Rather than return to the house and risk seeing him again, she reviewed her plans for the ranch and the details she still needed to resolve regarding the possible expansion of her business.

Her thoughts kept circling back to the present situation.

What was she going to do with Jared?

It was late afternoon when hunger could no longer be ignored. She had to return to the house, the house he was still in and get something to eat. She had lots to do before nightfall. Because of Jared's unexpected arrival, she'd wasted this afternoon.

Tomorrow she'd continue to clean the house, ignore Jared and put the place in shape for her business. She needed to make a list of repairs and architectural changes she wanted for a tearoom. She hoped she'd find a local contractor who wouldn't charge a small fortune.

It was quiet when Kelsey entered the kitchen. She paused, head cocked, listening for Jared. No sounds disturbed the silence. Almost tiptoeing, she crossed to the refrigerator. She'd planned to have a salad with some fresh-made bread. A slice of spice cake for dessert would finish the light meal.

As she cut and diced vegetables for her salad, she

wondered if she should fix enough for Jared. It wouldn't be any extra trouble. She wanted to stay aloof.

But she didn't want anyone to go hungry. Even her worst enemy.

If by giving him a meal he thought it meant she'd changed her mind she'd soon set him straight.

Almost finished with the salad, she popped the bread into the oven to warm.

"Need help with anything?" Jared's low voice from the doorway made her jump.

"No. I'm fixing a salad for dinner. You're welcomed to have some of it if you like."

If it wasn't something he wanted, she'd suggest he drive back to town and find a place to eat there.

Her expression brightened at the thought. Maybe she should suggest it.

"Sounds fine. I ate a big meal before leaving Dallas," he said.

Jared leaned against the door-frame his arms folded across his chest as he watched her while she worked, his gaze roaming down the slim, tanned legs that showed beneath her shorts, to the cotton shirt that had the top two buttons unfastened, at her blonde hair, a curly mop framing her glowing skin. She still fascinated him.

He'd heard nothing from her in four years. Nor any updates from family members—except his mother. And her vague Kelsey's doing fine never satisfied the curiosity he'd burned with.

He should have come back sooner. He should have forced the issue long before now.

Water under the bridge. He was here now.

Kelsey grew self-conscious as she worked. He wouldn't stop looking at her. His staring made her nervous and, since that was undoubtedly his purpose, she ignored him as much as possible. That was easier said than done. Every nerve-ending screamed for relief and she wished she dare grab her food and escape to her room. Away from his disturbing presence.

He was deliberately trying to provoke a reaction from her.

And she refused to give in to it.

Her nerves were drawn taut, almost to the snapping-point. Why wouldn't he go back to wherever he'd been and let her eat her meal in peace? She saw him from the corner of her eye, his hair still tousled –from running his fingers through it? It was another trait she remembered from before.

His body was trim and fit—no spare fat on Jared Martin. He had to keep in shape—the camera would capture any deficiencies. Even as a kid he'd been conscientious about taking care of himself.

She closed her eyes, trying to block out the images of him that flooded her memory.

At last the bread was ready. Kelsey heaped the salad on her plate, took the warm bread from the oven and sliced it into generous portions. Filling a plate for Jared, she left it on the counter, motioning to him to help himself. She wasn't going to hand it to him. She didn't want to come that close.

The amusement in his eyes told her he knew exactly why she'd refused to hand him the plate. Tossing her head, she walked down the hallway and out to the front porch.

Jared had brought two dining-chairs to the porch. They were together near the railing. With a quick glance, Kelsey went to sit on the top step, as she had the previous two days since she'd arrived.

She loved the late afternoon. It was peaceful and serene and the view spread out before her was one she'd never tire of. The rolling fields, the distant mountains and the brilliant blue sky were so different from the views she saw in Dallas. It was beautiful country, this part of Texas.

When Jared came out he paused, noting her rejection of the chairs.

Kelsey held her breath. Would he come and sit beside her on the steps? She couldn't stand to have him so close. The seconds stretched out. It was all she could do to keep her eyes on her plate. What was he doing? Slowly she let her breath go when she heard his footsteps move towards the chairs.

Kelsey ate her dinner, ignoring him, gazing over the fields of grass, cattle visible in the distance. She enjoyed the late afternoon sun and the balmy breeze that was now stirring. The air was warm and humid, caressing her cheeks as she sat on the step. The weather was beautiful, perfect, though rain was expected in the next day or two. She'd plan her renovation activities to accommodate the weather. Indoors when it rained, outdoors when it was fine.

"The bread's good—did you make it?" Jared's voice broke into her reverie.

"Yes, thank you."

She could at least be polite. Even for Jared.

"Tell me more about your plans for this place," he invited as the silence stretched out.

She swung around to look at him suspiciously. "Why?"

What did he want? Why did he care?

He shrugged. Finishing the last of the bread he put his plate on the chair next to him. He tipped back his chair and crossed his feet on the railing.

"If we don't sell, then I want details of what you plan on doing here. It's half mine, you seem to forget."

"I never forget! I don't understand why Uncle Henry left it to both of us," she blurted out. It'd been a sore point since she'd heard of the legacy.

"Me neither, but he did. If I can't sell I might as well make the most of it and help with fixing it up."

She stared at him in shock which turned to suspicion. She narrowed her eyes as she stared at him. It was the last thing she expected—or wanted. What was he up to?

"I don't want you here," she said.

"Too bad. This place's half mine. If any work gets done, I help."

"I want it for Grandma's. You don't want it or need it. You have all that money from your movies. Don't do this, Jared."

Kelsey had a deep, dark premonition. If Jared stayed he'd ruin everything. She needed this place. He was throwing his weight around, being as much of a pain as he could be.

"Do what, my sweet? Stay and see that my interests are protected. Surely that makes business sense."

"Don't you have a movie to start in?"

"I'll be starting another one in a few months. I'm between now. Plenty of time to stay and help out around here."

He looked out over the weed-choked yard to the fields beyond the drive. At least the fencing seemed strong and substantial from where he stood.

"You wouldn't be a help," she muttered, furious with the turn of events.

Was there any way to get rid of him?

"Tell you what, Kel. I'll stay and work with you on fixing this place up. At the end of the project we'll get someone in to value it and you can buy my half if you still want to. I'll even make terms for you, if you need it."

"Why don't you do that now?"

"I've got time between films. I'm at a loose end. It's be something different from what I've been doing."

He made it sound almost reasonable. There had to be more. What had he been doing between filming these last years?

What about his earlier statement about claiming his wife? Where did that fall into this new plan of his?

Wife? Not ex-wife? Why hadn't she picked up on that earlier?

She swung around to face him.

"Jared, did you ever finalize the divorce?"

He studied her a moment, his eyes guarded, his face expressionless. He shook his head.

"Why not?"

She was stunned. She thought the legal aspect had been handled years ago. What if she'd gotten married again? Not that that was likely, but still—

He turned away and remained silent so long that Kelsey thought he wouldn't answer. But when he spoke he chose his words carefully.

"It suited me not to, I suppose. We need to discuss the whole situation, Kelsey. You were wrong."

"Don't bring it up, Jared. I don't want to discuss it. I know what I saw. I thought you'd get a divorce first thing. I signed all the papers."

"I thought you'd at least listen to me. Your lack of trust hurt, Kelsey." He was silent for a moment, then shrugged. "Maybe I wanted the protection being married gives. Whatever happens, no one expects marriage from a guy who's already married."

"So it was insurance against becoming entangled with all the women you—"

She stopped, unable to go on, ignoring his desire to talk about what happened. It was over long ago. She'd moved on.

Yet the hurt was overwhelming, even now.

She stood up and turned to go back inside.

"Slept with, is that what you're thinking?"

His chair rocked down on all four legs and he stood up glaring at her.

She tilted her chin, "Yes, that's exactly what I'm thinking!"

"Well, I didn't, not that it's any of your business. You made that perfectly clear at the time. You don't want to know what happened. You just wrapped yourself up in your sanctimonious rightness and went your merry way.

19

But I haven't slept with anyone in years! Not since you, my sweet."

"That doesn't sound like the Jared Martin I discovered that morning in London. Not that I believe you. You probably discount them because they 'didn't mean a thing'!"

She stumbled towards the door, tears flooding her eyes, blurring her vision. She wouldn't break down before him, she vowed. Never again!

She pulled open the door and fled down the hall, her heart aching in fresh pain, wishing he'd never come.

Her life had been going fine until today.

She was shocked to discover that there among the few things in life that never changed, like the sun rising every day and the perpetual ebb and flow of the sea, was her love for Jared Martin.

Two

Kelsey tidied the kitchen then crept up the stairs to her room. She had no desire to spend another minute around that infuriating man. Maybe things would look better in the morning, after the shock of seeing him wore off. After a good night's sleep.

She dressed for bed in her short cotton gown. White and sleeveless, it was comfortable and cool in the hot night.

How soon could she get an air conditioning unit for the bedroom? And she'd want one for the kitchen. Or should she go ahead and do the whole house? A tearoom would need to be comfortable for guests.

Grabbing her Kindle, she climbed into bed and began to read. Minutes passed. Kelsey frowned. She was still on the same page. Why couldn't she get involved in the story? The book was by one of her favorite authors and she'd been so excited when she'd seen it on sale.

The reason, of course, was downstairs, still on the front porch for all she knew.

It was impossible to ignore the fact Jared was here.

She looked up when she heard the front door shut and steps on the stairs. In only a moment there was a perfunctory knock on her door and Jared pushed it open, standing in the frame, staring across the room at her.

"This room's taken. Get another," she said, resisting the urge to draw the sheet up to her neck.

Her heartbeat sped up and her throat became dry. The gown was sufficient covering, though she felt vulnerable and exposed lying in bed with the sheet covering only her legs.

She remembered other nights when he'd join her in bed. Crazy, wild, passionate nights. For an instant she wondered if he'd come to re-create one of those nights.

He studied the room, the threadbare rug, the colorful quilt bunched at the bottom of the bed, the pristine white curtains at the windows, washed just that morning.

"And which room would you suggest? When I looked through the house this afternoon, everything was dirty."

"If you'd done something about it then, you'd have a clean room tonight. First thing I did when I arrived two days ago was to fix up this room. Then cleaned the kitchen. I didn't sit gazing off into space all afternoon."

"Nor did I, little cousin. I spoke to Jim Harness, the foreman. Got information on the ranch, gave him a few directions. He's been waiting for someone to talk to. You've ignored him."

Kelsey sat up at that.

"I've ignored him! I like that. I've tried to find him for two days. Just like a man to wait until another man arrives. Go sleep with the cowboys—you're not sharing my bed."

He smiled sardonically and moved back to the hall. "You used to like it, as I recall."

Jared slowly shut the door. Maybe there was hope after all.

Would she become so angry if she were indifferent?

Today's arrival hadn't gone at all as he'd hoped.

He walked down the hall and looked into one of the other bedrooms. He wouldn't be surprised if there were bugs in the mattress.

He'd screwed up royally and it didn't look as if time had eased that wound.

He turned and went back downstairs. It was hot enough to sleep outside. And the porch was a better alternative than any of the mattresses in the house.

Kelsey stared at the closed door, her hands clenched into fists. She didn't love him. How could she have thought such a thing? Flinging herself back on the pillows, she closed her eyes tightly, willing away the images that danced behind her lids.

He was right, darn him! She'd loved sharing his bed, sharing his life. She'd loved him so much. In her fairy-tale world that love wouldn't have ever dimmed. It'd never have to stand the test of hardships and tragedy.

He'd betrayed that love.

For that she couldn't forgive him.

Kelsey tossed the Kindle on the bedside table and switched off the light.

But sleep proved elusive.

Lying in the dark, she tried to ignore the fact that Jared had come to disrupt her life, but nothing worked. Finally she resorted to reviewing all the steps she needed to take to update the old house into a charming tearoom and modern commercial kitchen she wanted.

If she couldn't sleep, she could be productive. Every time dark eyes danced before hers, she'd turn over on her other side and concentrate on all the steps to get her business set up at Windhaven Ranch. It was almost dawn before she slept.

Rhythmic pounding woke Kelsey in the morning. The sun was pouring in through her window, already promising another hot day. The air was still, the noise of the hammer traveling clearly to her room. She lay in bed for a moment, trying to place what she was hearing. It sounded like nails being pounded into wood. On the porch.

She sat up.

Feeling a desperate need to hurry, she quickly showered and donned shorts and a sleeveless cotton top. It was too hot for anything else. Dashing a brush through her curls, she was glad she'd cut her hair recently. The air was more humid here than in Dallas, too humid to have a length of heavy hair down her back.

She ran lightly down the stairs in bare feet and went to the screen door to peer out.

Jared had his back to her, setting in a new wooden board on the porch, one of the cowboys helping. To one side a stack of lumber stood ready. Placing the nails in the wood, Jared began pounding it into the porch.

From the number of new planks on the porch, he'd been doing it for a while.

Kelsey stood mesmerized. He wore shorts and tennis shoes. His skin was deeply tanned and his muscles moved sleekly, rhythmically, beneath that tanned skin as he raised and lowered the hammer.

His body was a work of art and she watched for endless minutes, remembering the texture of his skin beneath her fingertips, the mat of hair on his chest pressed against her breasts, the strength of his hands, their gentleness when making love to her.

Her hands clenched in remembrance, in longing.

Drawing a sharp breath at the direction of her thoughts, Kelsey spun around and walked away from the man who had caused her so much heartache. Away from the temptation to watch him and remember. There was no future in that.

Entering the kitchen a moment later, she saw that coffee had been made, but there were no signs of dirty pans or dishes. Had Jared not eaten anything for breakfast?

She pulled some cinnamon buns from the freezer— she'd heat them and have them and fruit for breakfast. Hesitating only a moment, she drew out enough to share with Jared and his helper.

Cutting up kiwi, banana and passion fruit, she rehearsed in her mind how she'd propose they work things out. She'd point out reasonably that it was impossible to stay together—it'd cause gossip that wouldn't be good for either of them. He'd made his choice clear years ago. He needed to leave.

She'd see if she was able to buy him out.

She'd be rational, calm and poised—show him she'd matured since he'd known her. She was no longer the adoring distant cousin he spent summers with from childhood. Nor the naive, adoring wife he'd so carelessly pushed aside four years ago.

She was a mature adult, capable of directing her own life and not waiting for scraps of love from a wanderer.

She put on a fresh pot and soon the aroma of the fresh-brewed coffee and the delicious fragrance of the buns filled the kitchen.

She placed the bowl of fruit in the center of the table, set three places and waited for the buns to finish heating.

"Something smells good."

Jared walked into the kitchen, smiling easily. His shorts rode low on his hips, his strong, flat stomach muscles corded as they disappeared into the cotton shorts. His legs were brown, as was the skin on his chest and arms.

His smile was the one Kelsey called his heart breaker. It had broken hers.

"Cinnamon buns. Fruit. Coffee. You got up early."

She had to force her eyes away. Good heavens, he was as sexy as ever.

"Not really—you slept in."

She glanced at the clock. He was right. But it was because she'd fallen asleep so late.

Not that she'd tell him that or the reason why.

"There's enough for your friend," she said as she pulled the hot buns from the oven, ignoring the implied criticism.

"Billy!" Jared roared, not moving. "Chow!"

He laid the hammer on the counter by the sink and washed his hands before pulling out a chair. Sitting, he studied Kelsey as she put the rolls on the table.

In a moment the cowboy appeared. He hesitated at the door.

"Good morning, I'm Kelsey Adams." Kelsey smiled at him and motioned to the table. "Did you have breakfast?"

"Good morning, madam. I ate before, but this sure looks good." He hesitated a moment.

"Sit, Billy, and we'll let Miss Adams tell us what she wants done around this place," Jared said.

Kelsey looked up at his tone. Had the use of her maiden name rankled?

Good. She'd been using it since they separated.

And, she'd thought their divorce final.

She smiled sweetly figuring that'd annoy him further. She reached for the fruit bowl. Maybe now he'd realized that she'd changed.

And that she wouldn't put up with him and his silly games.

As they ate Jared was the one who told Billy what needed to be done. Kelsey listened as he talked about repairing the porch, cleaning the yard, painting the exterior.

She was supposed to be in charge, yet he never asked her anything. She wouldn't argue with his plan, however. It was exactly what she wanted.

Listening to him, she remembered. How many times has she sat and listened to him when they were growing up? It was like Jared to take charge.

She'd heard that he even suggested changes to the directors of his films, suggestions that were usually followed. Did he really do that?

For the second time since he arrived she wondered what he'd been doing these last few years when not filming. Had he missed her at all?

She remembered the aching nights and dull days that followed their split. She'd wanted–

It didn't matter. The past was best left there. She had plans for her future. And they most certainly didn't include Jared.

"That's a start," she said, interposing herself into the discussion.

She didn't dare let Jared forget who was supposed to be running this. "I need to hire a contractor to discuss the renovation of the front rooms to make a tearoom. And the installation of commercial equipment in the kitchen."

"Where are you going to muster the cattle if you plan to have tourists coming to a fancy tearoom?" he asked.

"I want the ranch to continue as it has been. What do you mean?"

"Have you ever been around when they gather the cattle for sale?"

She shook her head.

Billy hid a smile behind a cup of coffee. His eyes laughed over the rim.

"It's messy and noisy and stinks. Not too conducive for the ambiance of a tearoom."

"Then I'll farm that out to a neighbor or someone."

"Not my half, you won't," he said smoothly.

Kelsey sat back, staring at him.

"Think again, sweetheart. The value of this ranch comes from its being a working cattle ranch, not as endless acres of land sitting fallow. If this venture of yours doesn't pan out you'll want to sell and it'll bring a better price if it's still a functioning cattle ranch."

"This 'venture of mine', as you call it, not only will pan out, but succeed even more than the last few years. This is not some fly-by-night operation. Grandma Mary's Cookies is already a success. This will ensure that it continues while enabling me to expand."

She was annoyed that he'd dismiss her business as inconsequential. Didn't he give her credit for anything?

Or did he still see her as the starry-eyed young girl who had adored him? The young woman he'd thought to dupe and then continue on as if nothing had ever happened.

He swirled his coffee gently in his cup, his eyes on the dark brew. Flicking a quick glance at Kelsey, he unloaded his next bombshell.

"In fact, I want to see what I can do to turn this ranch around. Make it profitable again."

She stared at him, dumbfounded. Was he serious? Yesterday he was talking about selling. Now he wanted to make the ranch profitable?

The man was an actor. One of the most successful ones in the business. Not some cowboy.

She didn't for an instant believe he wanted to become a Texas rancher. He wouldn't give up the fame and fortune, the adoring fans. Never give up the adoring women who flocked around him at parties and opening nights. Especially to run a ranch he knew very little about.

Uncle Henry had ranched all his life and let it go the last few years. It was hard, constant work.

No, he was trying to annoy her. Infuriate her, would be more like it.

When she remained silent, staring at him, Jared put down his coffee and tilted back in his chair, his dark eyes watching her, his mouth twitching as if to keep a smile at bay. He sat waiting for her reaction.

"In fact, Kelsey, under the terms of the will we inherit this place jointly. Nothing says you get the house, not the entire house."

"Now what are you doing? I've made plans and now you're trying to ruin them. Haven't you ruined enough in my life without this? You don't want this place. You'll be bored without the bright lights and adulation that goes with your job, your lifestyle, bored in a week. What game are you playing?"

"No game, sweetheart, maybe a change of heart."

He rocked down sharply on the chair and leaned towards her. He was so close that Kelsey felt the stirring of air as he breathed out, see the tiny lines that fanned out from his dark eyes, feel the heat from his body.

"I told you, I want my wife back. And I think, I hope, eventually she'll come back."

"Forget it."

She tried to look away from the piercing gleam of his eyes. But couldn't break the pull of attraction. Unwanted, the thought popped into her mind of how sexy he looked sitting at the table with his tanned chest only inches from her, the muscles sculpted and firm, his masculinity almost a tangible thing.

But she refused to go down that road again.

"Then I'll stay here and become a rancher."

"That's an empty threat," she said, wondering if it really was, feeling sick at the thought that he might carry it through.

"Is it?" His voice was silky, smooth, with enough amusement in it to make Kelsey wonder if he'd do it just to spite her.

"What do you want?" she asked flatly.

"I told you."

"No."

He sighed slightly and glanced at Billy, steadily eating, his eyes on his plate and cup, prudently ignoring the discussion swirling around him.

"Then we divide it front to back. You can have the kitchen. Or we could do it side to side," he suggested, watching her from the corner of his eye, waiting to see her reaction.

"No! I need the whole first floor for the tearoom and I planned to live upstairs. Blast it all stop this. I'll buy you out and you can head back to LA."

"I'm not going, Kelsey," he said, determination strong in his voice. "At least, not alone."

She stood abruptly and sped down the hall and out to the porch, stopping by the support pillar, leaning against it as she gazed with unseeing eyes over the ranch.

She seethed with anger.

He couldn't do this to her. He couldn't! She'd been planning on moving Grandma's here since she'd heard of Uncle Henry's death and that she'd inherited the ranch. It'd be perfect.

If she could buy Jared out and have nothing further to do with him.

Now he was threatening everything. Why? Why would he do this? She hadn't hurt him, it was the other way around.

Her throat ached with unshed tears, her eyes burned and her heart pounded in the apprehension that he'd ruin this part of her life, the way he'd ruined the rest.

Couldn't he leave her alone?

She'd never done anything except love him. Why was he so determined to challenge her?

"Kelsey?"

He joined her on the porch, close, but not touching.

"Go away, Jared. Please, go away." She trailed off in a whisper.

"Kelsey, my next picture won't start filming for another few months. I want to get to know you as you are today. Have you know me. See what might happen. Let's talk about what happened. I can explain. We can go forward from this point."

She turned to look at him as scornfully as possible. "Why? Does the famous actor want to make another conquest? Before moving on to the next woman? I'm not interested."

"You jumped to a wrong conclusion. Aided, I know, by Sally. And I reacted badly. But four years is enough!"

"So you say."

"I do say. Are you calling me a liar?"

"As well as a cheat, do you mean?" she spat out. "I don't think about you at all, if you want to know the truth. I avoid tabloids that might have any articles on you, never go to your movies. I don't care about you at all."

Liar, her conscience said. You think about him off

and on, mourn the loss of your marriage and wonder endlessly what you might have done differently.

"That's a low blow, Kelsey. I'm not a cheat and I'm not a liar, whatever you think. Listen to my explanation and don't be such a harsh judge. I'm only human. As you are. Give us another chance, Kelsey. What we had was good. It can be good again."

"No."

She looked away, over the pastures stretching to the horizon. The blue sky was cloudless, the sun hot and brassy as it climbed towards its zenith with no breeze to ease the heat.

The hurt in her heart was a steady ache. Four years wasn't long enough to erase that pain.

The moments ticked by, awareness of Jared uppermost in her thoughts. Why wouldn't he leave her alone?

"Truce, then." His voice was quiet.

"Truce?" She looked back.

"Yes. I stay for the next couple of months. We work to get this place fixed up the way you want for your bakery business and we see where we are at the end of two months."

She studied him for a few moments, looking for the catch in the plan.

Why was he suddenly changing his mind? Why was he now willing to help her, rather than stick to his tactic of keeping his half of the legacy separate?

Suspicious, she wondered what he was up to.

"At the end of two months you'll leave?"

She wanted the terms clearly stated.

"If you want me to."

"I do."

She was sure of that. In fact, she wasn't sure she'd last the two months.

"We'll fix the house up for Grandma Mary's Cookies?"

She wanted to be sure she understood exactly what he was proposing, even though she still didn't know why he was doing it.

"Yes. We'll fix the house up with a commercial kitchen and a tea room. But I'm serious about trying to pull a profit as a cattle ranch. I'll worry about that side, you take care of Grandma's."

Kelsey tried to see the catch, but she didn't.

"I don't have a choice, do I?" she asked.

"Not really. Uncle Henry did leave the place to jointly to us."

At least he was honest about it, Kelsey thought.

It'd mean putting up with him for two months.

It'd also mean no further worry about being able to do what she wanted. He wouldn't interfere and she could move ahead with her plans.

He'd offer help and in two months he'd be gone. With both of them working, things would get done faster. With that end goal in mind, it was worth the risk.

She frowned slightly at the thought of two months in close proximity with Jared. She didn't want to be around him. She did much better when he was thousands of miles away. How would she endure two months of seeing him every day? Remembering the happier times and then the reality of today.

Even if it meant she had the house without arguments in the end, and life could get back to normal, dare she try it?

"All right," she said at last, hoping she wasn't making a big mistake.

"There are terms," he said.

She tensed up.

"Like what?" she asked.

"Like no sniping. We work together in this. Harmoniously."

"Hah," she muttered, a mutinous look descending on her face.

He reached out and snared her chin in his fingers, tilting her face up towards him, leaning closer until he filled her vision.

"No sniping! We pretend we're distant cousins who haven't seen each other for a few years. We inherited this place together, so let's work together to get it on its feet again."

Kelsey thought she'd drown in the deep, dark brown of her cousin's eyes. His gaze penetrated the very core of her being, melting the ice that had encased her and warming her through and through.

She'd have agreed to anything he said at that point. The warmth of his fingers tingled along her jaw, evoked memories of long ago, and the love she'd had for her cousin Jared.

Could she do it? Could she pretend the awful past had never happened? Live and work with him for two months on the inheritance they'd both received?

If only—

Jerking her head from his hand, she took a step back to put distance between them, to try to gain perspective.

"Okay, no sniping. But we agree on things before we do anything. I don't want your cattle interfering with my tea shop."

Jared frowned slightly when she stepped back, but shrugged and moved to lean casually against the railing.

"Think of it as an added bonus. It'll lend even more authenticity to Grandma's image. A real working cattle ranch. You can add that to your tour."

She tilted her head in consideration. He made a good point. Foreign visitors especially liked touring a working ranch. It might add to the appeal of Windhaven.

Nodding, she agreed, then glanced around.

There was so much to do that she didn't know where to start. For a moment she let herself be glad that Jared'd be helping. It was monumental.

Yet in two months of both working together, it should be close to completion. Then he'd leave and she'd get on with her plans and her business and her life.

"Another term," Jared said from his position on the rail.

"What? You can't keep adding terms as we go along."

He looked at her and smiled. "One more. You do the cooking."

Kelsey smiled at him, suddenly convinced that things would work.

"Fine. I like to, after all."

"Those buns you made this morning were great. Now that we have things settled, I'll have another."

"We need to plan what to do and get started. I'm

running my company long-distance as it is. The sooner I can get it moved here the better," Kelsey said as she led the way back to the kitchen.

Billy had gone but not before finishing most of the cinnamon buns. Jared ate the last one while Kelsey cleaned up the breakfast dishes.

She took a pad of paper and found a pencil in a kitchen drawer. Sitting at the table, she looked at Jared.

"So we begin where?"

An hour later they'd listed all Kelsey wanted done around the house and Jared was on his way to the hardware store in town to order the supplies they'd figured they needed for some of the repairs he planned to handle.

Anxious to begin, Kelsey started clearing one of the downstairs rooms while he was gone. Thinking back over their conversations since he'd arrived, she wondered if their truce would work or if the past would rise up to interfere.

She'd do her part to keep things on an even keel. The list of changes and repairs was daunting. She'd value his help—if in fact he helped.

At the first sign of slacking off, she'd send him packing. Or leave herself.

Kelsey was well into stripping the old and faded wallpaper from one wall of the front room when Jared returned. He joined her and they worked silently, spraying the old paper with solvent, peeling it off the wall when it loosened. The soggy pile of wallpaper grew in the middle of the room, to be trashed later.

The day was muggy, the air still. Working in the room

was hot and messy. Kelsey brushed the perspiration from her eyes, blotting her cotton shirt against her body. She couldn't wait to finish and take a cool shower.

She paused at one point and surveyed the room. Still another two walls to go. They couldn't possibly finish before lunch, and she was almost too tired to eat as it was. Rotating her shoulders to ease some of the ache, she looked over at Jared.

He worked at the opposite end of the room. She watched him for a few minutes, admiring the way his muscles moved as he reached up for a strip of soggy wallpaper and peeled it down. She sighed unconsciously and tried to ignore the fluttering feeling within her. He was a gorgeous man.

They paused briefly for lunch—sandwiches made with some of Kelsey's homemade bread. Beer for Jared, lemonade for Kelsey. Then it was back to work. Both were eager to finish the stripping of the first room in preparation for the next step.

As the afternoon wound down, they approached the last section of wall. Kelsey was glad they were almost finished. She'd found herself wondering more and more about Jared as the day progressed, her curiosity constantly revolving around him.

Had he meant it when he'd said he could explain? Could anything make a difference to what she'd seen?

What had he been doing the last four years?

Why was he really here? To annoy her or to safeguard his inheritance?

As they drew closer and closer, stripping paper off the final wall, she became more and more aware of him, the strength of his muscles, the way he moved. She tried to ignore him, but she couldn't.

Time and time again her eyes drifted to him, watching him for brief seconds, then snapping back to the task at hand.

Had he noticed?

Soon one of them would have to stop—there'd only be enough wallpaper remaining for one person to strip.

Kelsey hoped she'd be the one to stop. She was exhausted. Her hands ached from the unaccustomed gripping of the paper to pull it down, her shoulders ached from scraping the residue from the plaster, and her legs ached from the constant up and down motion.

Jared's hand brushed lightly against her and Kelsey scrambled back as if she'd been burned, tripping over the rubbish and falling heavily on her bottom. She stared at him with wide-open eyes.

"What do you think you're doing?" she asked from the floor, glaring up at him as he stood over her, his legs spread, his arms hanging easily at his sides.

Amusement and something else lurked in his eyes as he watched her.

"I've been wondering all day if you were wearing a bra."

"You could have asked!" she snapped out, glaring at him.

"I didn't think you'd tell me."

"You're right. It's none of your blasted business!"

"Another term—no swearing. It's not nice on you."

"That's hardly swearing. Don't touch me again. Another term—no touching."

"Thought you didn't want terms added," he said lazily, his smile causing butterflies in Kelsey's stomach.

She pushed back a little and scrambled to stand up, as far from him as possible and still be in the same room.

"That's an important one. You finish up here. I'm going to get a bag for the trash."

Head held high, she marched from the room, her body almost trembling in reaction to his touch, the heated graze of his fingers against her still lingering.

Forgotten yearning arose, which Kelsey quickly damped down.

From now on, no touching—it was a term she'd insist upon. It was too dangerous otherwise.

Three

Kelsey took a refreshing shower, then went downstairs to the office. She spent the rest of the afternoon on business, talking first with her manager—her aunt Ellie.

When Kelsey first expanded Grandma Mary's Cookies" sales beyond the Dallas area, she'd needed help. She'd found it with her aunt.

Ellie was a widow with no children who had lived in Dallas all her adult life. It'd been to Ellie that Kelsey had gone when she'd left Jared.

Ellie had been happy to go into business with her niece, pleased to be needed. Two other women who worked with them during the week enabled them to manage the entire operation.

"What do you think now that you've seen it? Will we be able to renovate it enough to use it like you want? Does it have all the features we need in the kitchen or can we install the equipment without going too far into debt?" her aunt asked when Kelsey reached her.

"I think it'll work perfectly. But it's going to be a bigger job than I originally thought. I don't think Uncle Henry did a thing to keep this place up the last two decades. Plus, I originally thought about converting one of the out buildings into a large kitchen, but it's too far from the house. I don't want to be running back and forth. I might see about building a commercial kitchen as an add on on the back of the house."

Kelsey wasn't sure what would happen when she told Jared. The kitchen in the old house simply wasn't large enough.

More money she hadn't counted on spending.

"We stripped the old paper off one of the rooms downstairs today. The view from the window is amazing. It'll be perfect for the tearoom. It opens right out onto the porch. Tomorrow we'll do another room. By the end of the week we should be ready for the first coats of paint, then the wallpaper. I found some nice material in town for the curtains."

"Who's 'we' ? I thought you went up alone. Have you found a helper already?" Her aunt was sharp.

For a second Kelsey panicked. She didn't want the family to know Jared was at the ranch. The last thing she wanted was well-meaning family members urging them to reconcile.

Or worst, coming to the ranch to see Jared.

Would Ellie tell anyone? Probably not. She'd stood by her thus far, but Kelsey didn't want to have to explain even to her aunt.

It'd be far better if no one suspected Jared was here. He'd be gone soon. She hoped.

"Actually I have some help—you know, cowboys and all. It'll make the work go faster."

"What kind of help are they? Don't they just know

how to ride horses and brand cattle?"

"Give me some credit. I'm still finding out what he can do. But I know he's capable of basic things, like stripping wall paper and painting. If I need a specialist, I'll hire one. Anyway, we're moving right along. I wanted to check on the Markham deal. I'll call again in a couple of days."

"How long before you'll be ready, do you know?" Ellie asked.

"A couple of months at the earliest. In plenty of time for the first order to Markham, if we get that account. I'm still in shock they called us."

"Good products sell themselves. I've been telling you that."

The rest of the conversation concerned the new orders, how the different women who worked for Kelsey were coping with the increased demand and when Kelsey should start hiring workers for Windhaven.

"I'll come there when it's time. I can help with the interviewing and training the new women," Ellie offered.

"I'll keep you posted on the progress. For now I'm working on the front part of the house, getting it ready. I'll need professional help for the kitchen, however."

Kelsey reviewed some plans with her aunt before ending the call.

She'd been deliberately vague about details and knew she'd escaped detection so far. Ellie didn't know about Jared. His being here was awkward enough without any well-meaning interference from the family.

She stayed in the office, arranging her files, working on cleaning up the space, carefully putting the books and records concerning the ranch in a stack near the door. Jared might want to see them but she didn't want him in her office. The room wasn't large and his presence would overpower it. And her.

She planned to use the room as her office so Kelsey wanted to get it in order. She also wanted to avoid being with Jared.

As she cleaned, she heard pounding again. He must be back on the porch, repairing the rest of the sagging points. Painting the outside was one job Jared insisted he'd do, with the help of Billy and maybe some more of the cowboys who worked on the ranch.

Kelsey was glad to leave it to him. Especially if it kept him away from her.

When she finished in the office, she went to start dinner.

She liked to cook. She found it soothing and restful. It'd been the major factor in her starting Grandma's, the only thing she did well.

As she worked she listened to the muffled conversation between Jared and Billy, the sound interspersed with the hammering, the screech of rotten wood being torn up and the sound of new wood being cut.

Maybe it wasn't all bad that he'd shown up. She couldn't do the work he was doing and would have ended up spending even more money to get it done.

The sun was dropping in the back of the house as it set and added to the heat of the day. With the oven on and the sun shining in, the heat began to build.

Kelsey pulled her top away from her a couple of

times, trying to stir some air, cool her heated body. She should install air-conditioning in this room first thing. Texas was hot in summer. The high humidity made it more uncomfortable. The kitchen would be unbearable without some sort of cooling—even for fixing meals much less hours of baking the cookies.

Worry about the expense gave her pause, though. She couldn't afford everything she wanted. She'd planned on selling the cattle to bring some cash. If Jared wouldn't sell his half, would her half bring in enough to cover her expenses?

She made a fresh pitcher of lemonade and poured herself a large frosty glass. Hesitating only a moment, she grabbed a couple of glasses and the big pitcher. When she opened the screen door, the men were still hard at work and didn't see her at first.

"Lemonade?" she offered as the screen banged shut behind her. Try as she might, she couldn't keep her eyes from Jared. His shoulders were gleaming with a light sheen of perspiration. His muscles rippled beneath his skin as he stretched and rolled his shoulders to loosen some of the kinks. His stomach was taut, firm, flat. His shorts rode dangerously low on his hips. She blinked when she became aware of where her gaze had fastened.

His satisfied smile caught her eye and she looked away, flushing when she became aware that he'd seen her perusal. His knowing gaze angered her, but whether the anger was aimed at him or at herself she wasn't sure. He proved to be nothing but trouble. Why didn't he leave? Leave her alone and in lonely peace.

"Good idea, sweetheart. It's hot out here."

Jared tossed down the hammer and a handful of nails and reached for one of the glasses. Kelsey handed one to him careful that their fingers didn't touch.

Jared quirked an eyebrow at her, smiling at her obvious tactic. "Afraid?" he asked softly so Billy couldn't hear.

"Just following the terms," she sassed back, stepping widely around him, offering Billy lemonade with a wide smile. A smile that'd been missing when she'd spoken to Jared.

"Y'all have done lot. How soon will you be ready to paint?" she asked, looking at the improvement already evident in the porch.

Almost a quarter of the area had been repaired. She walked around on it, noticing how substantial it now felt. For a moment she was grateful to her cousin—she wouldn't have had the skill to do that. And hiring carpenters would have cost a pretty penny.

She wondered how much he agreed to pay Billy. They obviously needed to have another discussion—this time on how much money she had to spend so he didn't go hog wild and spend more than she could afford.

Curious, she glanced over, wondering where Jared had obtained the knowledge and skill to repair the porch.

"It won't be ready for a few days. I want to finish all the repair work around the house first. We'll work inside mornings when the sun's on this area, afternoons outside when this is the shady side of the house. When we move to the back we'll reverse the timing."

"You seem to have it all planned. How do you know so much about carpentry?" Kelsey asked.

He smiled easily. "Actors do a lot of other work when starting out. I use to work construction. Got more experience than I wanted—or thought I'd ever need. Who knew?"

She hadn't known that.

What else might she not know about him?

Jared leaned casually against the wall of the house, narrowing his eyes as he gazed out over the distant hills. A rainy spell had ended and the land bloomed in the new growth. Soon the hot sun would dry the grass and turn the land golden-brown. But for now the hills were soft and lovely in their green mantle.

In the distance cattle grazed on the lush grass. The setting was pastoral and reminiscent of early days in Texas.

The perfect setting for Grandma Mary's Tearoom.

"I'll talk with the cowboys tonight, work on the business end of the ranch in the evenings."

Kelsey nodded, glad to know she didn't have to worry about spending the evenings in close proximity with Jared. She felt unsettled.

Suddenly two months seemed endless.

"Supper soon," she said, carefully walking around Jared to reenter the house.

"Come tomorrow after lunch, Billy," Jared said, following Kelsey into the old farmhouse.

Conscious of his walking closely behind her, Kelsey kept her pace even as she moved down the hall, refusing to let his presence disturb her.

He veered off and took the stairs and in only a few moments Kelsey heard the shower as she shredded lettuce for a salad. Firmly turning her mind away from the image it held of Jared under the warm water, his hair even darker when wet, the slick film of water on his body, she tossed the vegetable into the bowl and began paring carrots.

Dinner was ready to dish up when Jared joined Kelsey in the warm kitchen some time later. He sat at the old round, scarred table, leaning back in his chair, watching her bustle around the old-fashioned room. The appliances needed updating. The entire house needed so much work. Had she realized what a job it'd be to bring this place up to code and make it appealing to tourists?

Her hair was fresh and clean, curling in the dampness of the humid air. He enjoyed watching her, despite her stand-offish manner. It was easy to get a rise out of her and she looked so beautiful when her eyes were flashing.

Kelsey did her best to ignore him as she put the food on the table, being careful not to come too close. She suspected he waited for a chance to touch her, to show that he wasn't bound by the terms of the truce, that he was above such things.

She wouldn't give him the chance.

They kept the conversation firmly on work yet to be done around the old ranch house.

"Tomorrow I want to check out the back yard to see if it's suitable for an addition for a commercial kitchen. That will take the most time to put in place and I'll need to order the equipment soon," Kelsey said as she spooned more vegetables on her plate. She wasn't going to give up on her plan, no matter what Jared said.

"How are you going to afford that?"

She shrugged. This was the dicey part. "Sell some

cattle, I guess."

"Now's not the time to sell."

"I can't afford to build kitchen without some influx of cash."

"Get a mortgage on your half of the ranch."

He helped himself to more meat.

Obviously the portion she'd given him wasn't enough.

Kelsey was fascinated by the amount he ate. There was no extra flesh on him at all, yet he ate huge meals. Where did he put it all?

"Though if your business isn't bringing in any money, why do you keep doing it?" he commented as he settled down to eat.

"It brings in plenty of money. Some of it I roll back to expand. I have a healthy bank account, just not enough to build a commercial kitchen from scratch. Not that it's any of your business," she said, defensive.

Why would he think she wasn't earning money? Did he believe her parents were still supporting her?

"In addition to what I send you or because of it?" he asked.

She stared at him, lowering her fork, puzzled.

"What do you send me?"

"The money I pay into our account each month."

Jared put his fork down and looked at her, his face hardening slightly in the glowing light from the overhead fixture.

"I don't know what you're talking about," she said, frowning.

It didn't make sense.

"The money in the checking account."

His spoke deliberately, like explaining things to a child.

"I have my own account and earned every penny in it," she said, tilting her head slightly with justifiable pride.

"The joint account we had," he explained patiently.

"I've never touched that since that morning in London. If you have money there, it's yours."

She resumed eating. At least she was clear on that.

"Kelsey, I've put money into that account every month for you."

She looked up at that. "Why?" Her eyes narrowed as she took him in. "Conscience money?"

"You're my wife, it's support money!"

"I didn't know that."

She sat back in her chair, her food forgotten. Despite herself, she was touched.

"I thought we were divorced."

"How can we be divorced? Did you ever get any final papers or anything? You can't get a divorce without signing papers all over the place."

Jared knew the answer—there had been no papers— but how could they be divorced without some sort of documentation? Didn't she have any sense?

"I don't know. I never got any, but for all I know you sent them to my parents' place."

"Wouldn't they have given you any papers when you visited?"

Kelsey dropped her gaze, looking at her plate, then at her glass of lemonade. Her heart constricted slightly.

"I haven't seen my parents since we split up," she said

slowly, softly.

"Good grief, why not?" Jared was astonished, then perplexed.

Kelsey was close to her family and his. They were third cousins once removed, had known each other all her life. While their paths hadn't crossed often as children, their parents were close. Hers lived in Galveston and his mother visited frequently. Their mothers were third cousins, but closer than some sisters.

"Reasons." She said vaguely, standing suddenly and clearing her place.

She moved to the sink and kept her back to him. There was no need to let him know how awkward she felt around her family after failing to keep her husband.

What did it matter? The situation wasn't likely to change.

"What reasons?" Jared loomed over her, moving quickly and silently across the room to stand close to her, hemming her in by the sink. His voice demanding.

He was used to getting his way in things and that tone of voice didn't bode well.

"Silly, unimportant ones, all right? Go on, I'll do the dishes. You go talk to the cowboys."

"I'm not leaving, Kel, until you tell me what I want to know."

"You'll grow old then," she said flippantly, and moved to get his plate from the table.

He didn't move. Kelsey eyed him as she approached. He stood too close to the sink for her to do the dishes, but she knew he wouldn't move an inch if she didn't tell him. Stubborn, infuriating man.

No wonder he was so good in the action films he starred in—his very presence intimidated.

Kelsey stood in indecision. Should she leave the dishes until morning or continue as if he wasn't there, as if his mere presence didn't destroy her last trace of patience.

"Kelsey."

It came out almost a growl. His eyes were narrowed and he tensed slightly. As if about to pounce, she thought fancifully.

"It's nothing. I'm a coward, that's all. There, are you happy? Now get out of my way!"

"You're the last person I think of if I think of cowards. What are you talking about?"

He didn't move.

"I didn't want to have to listen endlessly to their telling me I told you so. So I never went back."

"Who?"

"My mother, your mother, everybody. Go away, Jared. I want to finish cleaning up and go to bed. I'm tired from all I did today."

"Not until I know what you're talking about!"

He crossed his arms over his chest and leaned against the edge of the sink, his gaze never wavering from her face.

She hesitated, not wanting to admit it, but knowing that their mothers had been right all along. She'd been a hard-headed, stubborn fool. They deserved the opportunity to say, "I told you so," but she hadn't wanted to hear it. Still didn't want to.

"Neither your mother nor mine wanted me to marry

you. They tried their best to talk me out of it. They said you didn't really love me, only yourself. It suited you to marry me then, but I'd only end up unhappy. Well, they were right, weren't they? But I don't want it thrown up in my face all the time, so I don't go home."

She pushed past him and dumped the dishes in the sink, turning on the water.

"I can't believe that!"

He stared at her, shock evident in his expression.

"Believe it, it's true. But I was so crazy in love with you back then, I wouldn't listen." Kelsey said.

She should have listened. It'd have saved her so much heartache. Why didn't children understand that their parents often knew what was best?

"Two old-fashioned mothers what would they know?"

Jared's temper began to rise. He didn't like knowing his own mother had been against his marriage.

"A lot. I've thought about it over the years, Jared. You never once said you loved me. Never once. I've remembered all the times we were together, rehashed them over and over in my mind to find a single instance and never came up with a single one."

"That's stupid. Of course I did. Why else would I marry you?"

Jared's stance was rigid, controlled, his anger barely leashed. He'd been captivated by her since she'd been a teenager. Waited for her to grow up and delighted in knowing she wanted him as much as he wanted her.

She shrugged, rinsing a plate beneath the running water.

"It suited some purpose, I suppose. Anyway, I thought one of the terms of our truce was that we wouldn't bring up the past."

Kelsey wanted to forget everything about their past and concentrate on her plans to make the ranch the new production center for Grandma Mary's Cookies.

"This is the present. Do you still feel that way?"

His voice sounded hard, cold, controlled.

She looked up at him, saw the anger in his expression, his lips a tight line, his eyes glittering down at her, narrowed and hard.

Kelsey shivered slightly. "What way—about our mothers?"

"No, that I never loved you."

"It doesn't matter now. What we had ended years ago. You saw to that. Go away!"

She shoved him to get him to move away from her, to relieve some of the frustration and anger she herself felt when dealing with him.

"Ah, darling, one of the terms is no touching. You broke it—forfeit time."

His voice was hard, anger still riding him.

Before Kelsey moved, before she protested, he leaned over and kissed her on the mouth, his hands drawing her up against him.

The kiss was short, over almost before Kelsey knew what happened.

Her eyes widened in shock and she raised her hand to slap the triumphant grin from his face. But his hand caught her wrist, holding it only inches away from his cheek.

"Now, sweetheart, you keep doing that and I'll believe all you want is the forfeit. You broke a term of our truce. Keep touching me and I'll keep kissing you."

"Stay away from me and we wouldn't have this problem," she hissed through clenched teeth.

His grip was firm on her wrist. All Kelsey felt was a tingling awareness. And a curious longing deep within.

"I'm sure we'll always have this problem."

"But not if you left," she said, wondering if she really wanted him to go or stay the full two months.

"All in good time, sweetheart, all in good time."

His anger had abated and his touch gentled. His thumb traced lazy circles against the soft, sensitive skin of her wrist, causing shivers of awareness to course up through her arm, travel through her to touch the very core of her being.

Kelsey hesitated a moment. Did she want him to let her go?

Aware of where her thoughts were leading—appalled at where they were leading–she tugged.

Jared laughed, kissed her open palm and gently lowered her wrist, releasing her.

"Go see the cowboys and leave me alone!"

She turned back to the sink, longing to cradle her wrist against her breasts, dwell on the feel of his lips against her palm, the delight his touch wrought for a few, all too few precious moments.

He said nothing and Kelsey kept her eyes on the rising water in the sink as she listened to his footsteps stomp away. In only seconds she heard the throaty growl of his big motorcycle as it revved up and sped away through the night.

"He'll scare the cattle from here to New Orleans with that infernal machine," she mumbled to herself as she began washing. Already the night loomed long and lonely ahead of her.

Kelsey awoke shortly after dawn, having gone to bed early, convinced she wouldn't sleep a wink. But it'd taken her a short time to doze off and she'd slept the night through without waking and without dreams.

For a few moments she lay in bed, savoring the warble of the birds in the old oak trees. The tall old trees had been planted to provide shade for the house long ago when Uncle Henry's parents had first built it.

Kelsey smiled as she felt the cool morning air on her cheeks, the softly scented air filled with the pungent smell of cattle. It was as cool as it was likely to get today.

She hadn't heard Jared come home last night. Either she'd slept very well or he hadn't returned. It must be the latter—the motorcycle was too loud to ignore, even if asleep.

She quickly dressed in a cotton top and shorts.

She stole quietly down the stairs. If he came home it had to have been late. She wouldn't wake him. It was still early.

Opening the front door, she saw the big black bike parked beneath the nearest tree. He had returned. Why hadn't she heard him?

Kelsey slipped into the kitchen, wondering where

Jared had gone last night, and what he'd done. Had he only visited the cowboys?

Or had he gone into Willowby? There were a couple of bars there that catered for the locals—he might have passed time there. Anything rather than stay at home.

And why should he stay home? she asked herself as she pulled eggs and butter from the fridge. There was nothing to keep him here.

She wanted him as far from her as he'd go.

But she wouldn't have minded if he'd stayed and talked to her about Los Angeles. About what he'd been doing the last four years. If he had any regrets—

Slamming the bowl down, she turned her thoughts firmly away from the path they were following. She didn't care a penny for what he'd been doing. Probably sleeping with every starlet in Hollywood. The thought caused a sharp pain in her heart and she couldn't get the picture from her mind.

Four years ago she'd wanted to surprise her husband. They'd been married for only two years—and separated much of that time when Jared went on location for his filming. She hadn't minded. She'd been so proud of him. So proud of his ability as an actor. So proud of his meteoric rise from supporting actor to leading man.

Even when he'd accepted a part in a film that'd take him to Europe for six months, she'd been proud of him. And so happy.

His calls had become few and far between. Email was almost non-existent. Still, caught up in her happy bubble of love, she'd suspected nothing.

Booking a flight from Los Angeles to London,

keeping her visit a surprise, Kelsey arrived early one morning at the address of the small house he'd been renting.

Anguish gripped her as she remembered that morning. How stupidly naive she'd been. How dumb to think he'd be glad to see her.

She'd dismissed the cab and hurried up the walkway. When she'd rung the bell, she had been amused at how long it took to answer. Was she waking him up? Excitement had built as she'd waited to see him. Had he had a late night? Wouldn't he be surprised to see her?

But it had been Kelsey who'd received the surprise— shock rather. When the door had finally opened, it hadn't been Jared, but a pretty young woman, dressed in next to nothing!

Kelsey's heart raced as she remembered staring at her, wondering if she had the wrong house, knowing she didn't.

What was this woman doing in Jared's house early in the morning, with almost nothing on?

"Can I help you?" she asked.

"Is Jared Martin here?"

"You a fan?" she asked.

"No. I'm his wife," Kelsey said faintly. Surely she had the wrong house.

The other women's face lit up in malicious amusement. "Well, well, the missing wife. Jared's mentioned you. He's still asleep. Poor thing, we had a long day yesterday, and an even longer night."

She smiled slyly, staring boldly at Kelsey.

Kelsey felt sick. "Is he here?" she asked again.

The woman shrugged and nodded, looking up the wide stairs. "He's still in bed. Do you want me to wake him up for you?"

Kelsey took a deep breath and stepped inside the house. She'd see for herself.

"No, I can manage."

She climbed the stairs, the woman following right behind her. Kelsey tried to keep her eyes away from the skimpy attire, tried to keep calm and find a logical explanation for what was happening. When they reached the second floor, the woman dashed ahead of Kelsey and flung open the door.

Jared lay asleep in the big wide bed.

"Darling, we're found out," she'd called out gaily, laughing at Kelsey and dancing over towards the bed.

Kelsey could still see Jared's face when he woke. Seeing her, he went white, then flung off the covers and sprang from bed. Nude. She turned and fled. All the evidence had been before her eyes.

"Kelsey! What the hell is going on?" he called out, but she was already running down the stairs, out of the front door.

In a heartbeat her world had crashed down around her. If she'd had a second's doubt, the look on Jared's face as he ran after her, covered only with hastily pulled on jeans, would have convinced her.

Reaching the pavement, Kelsey began walking, her suitcase, snatched up in passing, dragging behind her, clicking on the cracks in the sidewalk.

"Kelsey, wait a minute." Jared hurried after her, grabbing her arm, swinging her around to face him.

She stared at him with disbelieving eyes. The husband she'd adored, betrayed her, their marriage. How could he?

"No, I won't wait. I'm going home. Goodbye, Jared."

"Kelsey, it's not what you think. I can explain—I think."

He frowned then and shook his head.

"Jared, your friend's waiting for you—probably in your bed!"

She jerked her arm from his grip and walked rapidly away. She'd dismissed the cab. She hadn't expected to need it. She thought she was going to stay with her husband not that she'd immediately want a ride back to the airport.

How wrong she'd been.

He winced. "Don't talk so loud. I have an awful headache."

"Too bad," she yelled, trying to keep from being sick, trying to keep some semblance of composure while her world spun out of control.

"I don't know why Sally's there."

"She said you'd had a busy night From her attire and your rumpled bed, I can just imagine."

He drew himself up and stared down at her, anger building despite the pain of his headache.

"Where's my loyal wife who believes in her husband? Isn't there any trust in this relationship?" he asked her, his voice hard.

"None! You've seen to that!"

Her hand ached. Glancing down in surprise, Kelsey saw that she clutched the counter-edge in a death grip. She took a shaky breath and eased her hold.

She hadn't thought about that awful day in months.

They'd made a truce to ignore the past. Not bring it up. She shouldn't be thinking about it now. She had lots of work to do to prepare the ranch for her business and no time to fret over what she couldn't change. No matter how much she'd longed to.

Baking soothed her, as it always did. She'd make enough rolls and bread to feed them for a week. She mixed the batter, poured the cakes, made rolls, breads and biscuits. Gradually the kitchen filled with the aromatic fragrance of baking cinnamon, allspice, nutmeg. The counters filled with cookies, cakes and rolls.

After stopping to cut a slice of fresh bread and butter it lavishly, she continued on. Soon the peace she'd found when she'd first arrived at Windhaven filled her.

"What time did you get up to do all this?" Jared's voice sounded in the doorway.

Kelsey turned, flicking her eyes over him, then back to the counter, loaded with fresh-baked goodies. She refused to let her guard down again. She'd remember the woman who'd greeted her that long-ago day and keep as far from him as possible.

"I woke early and thought I'd fix a few things to tide us over. I plan to work hard on fixing up this place. I need to get Grandma's moved so I can get back to my primary business."

"Which is baking. You can still do some baking here while we're renovating."

He moved easily across the room, stopping beside Kelsey, his eyes on the rolls and cookies cooling on trays.

He stood too close.

Kelsey eased herself a step to the left, trying to put more distance between them. She had difficulty breathing, and resolutely kept her own eyes on the result of her early morning work. Did he have any idea of the effect he had on her?

"There's more to it than merely baking. The kitchen here would have to pass health department inspection. Then there's packaging and distribution. I'd spend all my time on that, with none left to paint or paper. I've got people in Dallas working while I'm here."

"So this renovation is putting you behind at your work," he said, leaning against the counter laden with fresh-baked goods.

"A little. That's why I'm in such a hurry to get the house fixed up, so I can move the operations here. Which also depends on how fast I can get that commercial kitchen."

Kelsey was proud of what she'd accomplished after the devastating ending of her marriage. And she was glad that Jared would see how well she'd done without him, that she didn't need him any longer.

Four

"Are these for eating, or shipping out?" he asked, already reaching for the loaf of bread Kelsey had cut a slice from.

"For eating. Do you want some eggs for breakfast?"

She moved toward the fridge to put some distance between them. The sooner she fed him, the sooner he'd get to work.

"Sure. Bacon, too, if we've got any. This bread's super."

Kelsey nodded acknowledgment and set to work preparing breakfast.

"Plans for today?" Jared asked, leaning back against the counter and watching her.

He wore a navy blue T-shirt and his khaki shorts. His feet were still bare and he looked ready for anything.

"Work on stripping the paper in the dining room, I guess. Are you going to finish the porch?"

"We should be done this afternoon. I'll run a check on the rest of the house and plan to repair anything else in poor shape. I talked to some of the cowboys last night. They're willing to help paint the outside when we're ready. It'll go fast that way."

Kelsey's hopes rose. "Does that mean we'll be done in less than two months?"

"Are you trying to get rid of me?" he asked, his voice deceptively mild.

Of course, but he already knew that.

"In a hurry to get Grandma's going here," she said evenly.

He studied her for a moment, then shrugged. "I don't know. Depends on how much work remains. Who's minding the shop with you gone?"

"Aunt Ellie. She joined me about three years ago. She's the primary baker now. I bake, too, but usually I'm out selling, so she runs the production line. We have enough orders to keep us busy for the time being, but I need to get back out in the market to sell some more. While this time puts us behind a little, we'll be able to handle so much more once we have a bigger commercial kitchen."

"Only the two of you?" he asked casually, his attention focused.

He was definitely interested in learning more about Kelsey's business venture. She'd changed from the sweet, adoring young woman he'd married. She was more assured, more confident.

For a second his heart caught. What if what she said proved true—that she didn't want him anymore?

"We have a couple of women in Dallas who assist with the baking and packaging. That's enough until the orders expand. When we move here, I'm hoping to hire women from Willowby. It won't be a long commute for them and I'll pay market wages. Here are your eggs.

Coffee's ready, too."

She thrust his plate at him, almost dropping it in his hands as he reached for it to ensure that her hands didn't touch his.

She refused give any reason to repeat last night's forfeit.

"Aren't you eating?" he asked as he pulled out a chair and sat down.

"I've been sampling everything that's come from the oven. I'm full." She smiled ruefully.

"I don't need you waiting on me. If you weren't eating, I'd have fixed my own breakfast," Jared said, frowning.

She turned to look at him. "Well I'm not crazy about other people messing about in my kitchen. It suits me better to fix the meals whether I eat them or not, rather than have you rearranging how I have things set up."

"Yes, madam, boss lady," he teased her.

"Remember that if you're thinking of fixing a midnight snack or something," Kelsey ordered in mock-severity.

"Did you talk to the foreman last night about the cattle and the feasibility of running this as a profitable ranch?" she asked as she began washing up the remaining baking utensils.

"Sure did. Seems like it's easily handled. It's only been the last few years that Uncle Henry wasn't able to do all he should have. It won't take long, with careful management, to bring it back to a profitable enterprise. I'm going to ride out with Jim tomorrow to get an overview of the ranch. Want to come with?"

"Maybe. Are you going early?"

"Yeah, before it gets too hot."

"Who'll run the ranch? You'll be off making movies," she asked.

"I can keep an eye on it from wherever I am. Or you can since you'll be right here." He shrugged. "Jim'll do most of the work. We'll plan things out and he can manage things within certain parameters and then ask you or me for decisions if something comes up."

Kelsey tried to hide her dismay at his plans. Keeping this ranch going would mean he'd be constantly returning. She wondered how she'd cope seeing him from time to time beyond the next two months.

"Who's Jim?" she asked, refusing to consider beyond today.

Maybe he'd tire of the novelty and sell out. She could always hope.

"I told you, he was Uncle Henry's foreman."

"And he knows enough to run the entire ranch?"

"Yep. He kept it going the last few years when Henry was too sick to do anything. He can ramrod most of the day-to-day work with the cattle. We'd need to hire a business manager for that end of it or do it ourselves."

"I can't do it. I have another business to run. Why won't you consider selling the herd? Your life isn't even in Texas. You've lived in California for years. Why do you want ties here?"

Is it only to drive me to distraction? her mind screamed.

"While my work takes me all over, I don't have to live in LA when between films. Maybe I want to come back

66

to Texas. It's my home, too."

Her breath caught in her throat and it was a full minute before she spoke again.

"I'll start removing the wallpaper in the dining room. I'll break for lunch around one. If you aren't ready then, I'll leave you something," she said as she wiped the last crumbs from the counter.

Wrapping the food that had cooled, she felt all thumbs. She needed to get busy and keep busy. The sooner the house was completed, the sooner Jared would leave.

"Kelsey?" Jared called her name softly.

When she looked at him, he caught her eye, holding it for a long moment.

"Thanks for breakfast." His tone was soft, seductive, the Texas accent strong as ever.

"Sure."

She turned back to her task, her knees almost buckling beneath her. He was so darn gorgeous, his dark eyes like midnight on a stormy night, his teeth gleaming white against the deep tan. His voice caressing like dark velvet.

She finished wrapping the cookies while Jared finished eating. He carried his plate and fork to the sink, tossing them in carelessly and running water on them briefly. He turned and took a step towards Kelsey, the look in his eye intense.

Seeing him approach, she stepped back, to keep a certain distance between them. She didn't need the warmth of his body or the attraction of his smile, to ensnare her again.

"What's the matter, Kelsey?" Jared's mocking smile teased her as he deliberately took another step towards her.

She backed up until she was stopped by the coolness of the refrigerator door. Her gaze never left his. He was like a predatory creature, tracking her down, ready to pounce. Her heart sped up and pounded and her breathing became shallow.

"Jared..."

Before she told him to stay away, he closed the distance between them and leaned over to kiss her gently. His lips were warm and firm against hers, the kiss sweet and brief. A press of lips, a shock of awareness as the tip of his tongue brushed across her closed mouth, and he was done, straightening up and staring down at her.

"Thanks for breakfast."

Kelsey's eyes remained closed as she leaned back against the refrigerator, wanting to escape her memories, escape the feeling his touch brought, the yearning for the way things once had been. Trying to ignore how her heart was pounding, the blood rushing through her veins, the heat that built within her every time he touched her.

She opened her eyes, anger flaring as she remembered.

"Go find one of your starlets," she spat out, moving around him and storming out of the back door.

She was running away from Jared and his sweet kiss, from the temptation she seemed unable to resist. She knew trouble when she saw it, had recognized it when he arrived.

Why, then, couldn't she do something about it? She

thought she'd gotten over him. Why couldn't she resist?

Kelsey walked out into the morning sun—the heat already building. The day would end up as hot as the previous one.

She walked over to the large shade tree and looked around picturing an efficient commercial kitchen able to handle all the orders she'd get.

She wished Uncle Henry had left the ranch to one of them alone. If it had been to her, she'd have no problems. If to Jared, she'd never have known about it. Either way would have been preferable to the current situation.

There was plenty of room to erect a commercial kitchen, but the expense would be high. She leaned against the trunk of the oak. If she built a kitchen beneath these trees, it would have shelter from the sun during the hottest part of the afternoon. And it was close to the house, making it easier to go back and forth. It was a good location.

She sighed. Good location or not, without some way to raise a lot of money in a short time, she wasn't sure she could swing it.

One of her steadfast rules was not to get into debt.

Yet if they didn't have an expanded kitchen for higher productivity, there wasn't any advantage to moving from their current location.

And if she couldn't move the business here to Windhaven, what was the point of staying? The tearoom alone wasn't worth it. She wanted to add that to her current operation, but the primary goal had been to increase production to satisfy more markets.

Increase the business that way and sell all over the

western region. Maybe even nation-wide in time.

Her gaze roamed over the yard. The grass needed mowing, growing rapidly from the recent rain. The trees rustled softly with leaves moving slightly in the morning breeze. In the distance she heard the lowing of cattle, the sharp bark of the cattle dogs.

When her gaze settled on the old house, she stared at it for a long time. It needed so much work. There was no question about that. But she still relished the idea that had first come to her when she'd learned of Uncle Henry's bequest.

She wanted this to be the showplace for Grandma Mary's Cookies—an authentic farmhouse to support the image of Grandma Mary. Once fixed up, she'd use pictures of the house in promotional material.

And the only thing that stood between her and her goal was Jared Martin.

She pushed away from the tree and marched purposefully back to the house. She'd see the renovation through, figure out a way to build a kitchen, and see the back of Jared when she was finished.

He'd wreaked her life once before—she wouldn't let him succeed this time around!

Jared was already hard at work in the dining room, stripping paper from the walls. The windows were open to catch whatever breath of air stirred. The task before them was daunting, but he was working with a will to get it done.

She watched for a minute, before he realized she was

there, wondering why he was helping her? Why not let her do it all on her own?

Suddenly she wished she knew more about him. When had he worked in construction? Obviously before they married, but she didn't even remember hearing about it at family gatherings. What else had he done before making it big as an actor?

The superficiality of their one-time relationship was made clear by the fact she knew so little about him.

He turned to dump peeled paper and saw her. Cocking one eyebrow, he watched her silently for a moment.

"Planning to work today?" he asked.

Kelsey felt a warm tingle deep within. She didn't know why he was helping, but suddenly she was glad he was here, appreciated his help. Maybe she should take it at face value, use his help and say goodbye when he left.

"Isn't this the worst wallpaper you ever saw? No wonder people didn't like to eat here—it gave them indigestion," she said, moving into the room, ready to work.

Jared shrugged and turned back to the wall. "It looks like it was the original paper. In which case the first family here probably didn't have electricity, so couldn't see it most evenings. I know our founding forefathers were hardy stock. Even this wallpaper didn't faze them."

"I wonder how hard it was for them to come out here in the eighteen hundreds. Before roads or cars or the telephone were around," she mused as she started spraying the wallpaper, soaking a section in removal solution.

"Hey, I thought we weren't going to talk of the past," he said whimsically.

"That was our past, not history in general. Do you ever wish you lived back then?"

"Nope. I like the twenty-first century fine."

"I do, too, mostly. But there's a certain romance about the early days. When thinking about that time, I don't consider the conveniences not yet invented, but imagine the glamour of the era."

"What glamour? Lot of hard work, little return. Life expectancy short."

"I know—still, it holds some appeal. The country was young. Gold had just been discovered," she said scrapping the edge of the wallpaper. The strip was ready to be pulled off the wall.

"Still the romantic, eh?"

He dumped another soggy strip in the growing pile in the center of the room.

"I remember when you were about eight you loved the stories of the knights in King Arthur's court. Then as a teenager you and your sister use to drive me nuts when we visited, reading romantic stories and mooning about over the heroes."

Kelsey paused, remembering some of the visits he referred to. She even remembered the visit he was talking about, when she'd been soppy over dashing heroes of romance books. She'd secretly likened her heroes to her cousin. Even at thirteen, she'd already been captivated by Jared. He'd been twenty and at college. He'd thought he was so much more sophisticated than the two silly girls she and her sister had been back then.

Tears filled her eyes as she remembered that happy time. How bright the future seemed. How wonderful he seemed.

And how horribly things had turned out.

"Kelsey?"

She blinked, the tears spilling over, tracing tracks down her cheeks.

She didn't hear him move. The first indication she had was when he turned her around, his hands warm and gentle on her arms.

"Oh, baby, don't cry."

He cradled her cheeks, his fingers tangling in her curls, his thumbs brushing the trace of tears from her skin.

"I...I'm not. I got something in my eye," she lied.

Kelsey grabbed his wrists to bring his hands away from her face, to end the contact that was wreaking havoc with her senses. His fingers gently massaged her scalp, his thumbs brushing softly across her cheeks, like a butterfly's wing. His breath mingled with hers.

But when her fingers touched him she hesitated. She was aware of the strong surge of his pulse beneath her fingertips, the steady throb of his heart. The sudden longing to rest against him and absorb some of that strength was almost overwhelming.

"I told you no more touching."

She tried to sound stern, but the faint voice that came out hardly sounded like hers.

"I know and I broke the truce this time. So I must pay the forfeit."

So saying, Jared leaned over and captured her mouth with his.

His lips were gentle, but instantly aroused to passion. He molded her beneath him and then teased her lips until she responded.

Delight and desire exploded within Kelsey as she felt his kiss escalate. She tightened her grip on his wrists. Time stood still and Kelsey felt the pleasure throb through her, the feelings swamping her, desire rising.

Loosening her hands, she sought his shoulders, her arms encircling his neck.

Jared felt the change and moved to draw her into his arms, pulling her softness against his solid strength.

The strong muscles that embraced her heightened her enchantment as the world stopped and dream time surfaced.

When Jared moved to kiss her cheeks, to nuzzle her neck and trace fiery trails of kisses to that pulsating spot on her throat, sanity returned.

Kelsey shifted, aware of the danger of the situation, of the inappropriateness of her behavior, the wrongness of her reaction to the wonder of the kiss.

Horrified at her response, at the traitorous response she had to the man who'd betrayed their marriage vows, she pushed away in forceful denial.

"No!"

Wrenching herself from his arms, she stepped back a couple of steps, breathing hard, furious with him for his seductive ways, equally angry with herself for letting him get close to her, for giving in to his irresistible charm. It meant nothing. Nothing!

"It was just a kiss. You act as if I were going to attack you."

Jared turned away and picked up the sprayer, sending a stream of solvent along the wall.

She stood immobile, breathing hard, watching him. Only a kiss! She hadn't been able to last two days with him around. She'd never make it two months.

Longings and desires rose. Never extinguished, only dormant these last four years.

Yet to him it meant nothing.

She'd do well to remember that. She was merely one in a long line of conquests.

Slowly, with a wary eye, she moved back to her spot along the wall and began to peel the soggy paper. Licking her lips, slightly swollen from his kiss, she tasted him.

Her heart slammed against her chest and she clenched her teeth against the wave of desire that swept over her.

Enviously she noticed he worked without any problem, no regrets, no longings.

Blast it. Why couldn't he have been as affected by that kiss as she was? Another one like that and she'd be lost. Her careful reserve built up painfully over the last four years would be shattered and her heart would be open for more hurt.

She couldn't let that happen.

Jared worked in silence the rest of the morning, which suited Kelsey. She stayed as far across the room from him as possible totally concentrating on the task at hand. It was boring and monotonous work, but necessary to prepare the walls for the next step. She planned to get some bright cheery wallpaper. Something to match the homey feeling she wanted for Grandma's Tearoom.

The floors needed to be refinished. The trim painted, the lights replaced. And this was only one room.

Daydreaming about the changes she planned, she still kept a wary eye on Jared. Minutes before she planned to stop to fix lunch, he left the room without a word.

Kelsey didn't see him again until she had their lunch on the table—salad again with hot biscuits fresh from the oven. She was pouring herself a large glass of iced tea when he walked easily into the kitchen and slapped down a pad of paper before her.

Drawing out his chair, he began to eat, his eyes fixed on Kelsey.

"What is this?"

She looked at the pad. There were several notations on it, but at the bottom was a large number, underlined several times.

"That, my dear cousin Kelsey, is the amount of money in our account at the bank. More than enough to build your blasted kitchen."

He took a deep drink of his iced tea, never taking his eyes from her face.

Her startled gaze flew to him.

"That's not my money."

"It is."

"No."

"I deposited it for my wife. You're technically still my wife. The money's yours."

"I don't want it."

He shrugged and calmly continued to eat his salad. Only the slight tightening of his lips indicated that he was holding in his temper.

"I won't take it."

"Suit yourself."

He took another sip of tea and carefully placed the glass back on the table. Catching her eye, he continued, "But you don't have a lot of choices here, Kelsey. This ranch is half mine. I've granted you the right to fix up the house in any way you want. But that's all. I get half say in everything, and that includes keeping the cattle. If you're sincere in wanting to move your business here, you need to build a commercial kitchen. And you have the means to do it."

"With your money, you mean," she said bitterly.

"No, with your money. If you don't use it, it remains in the bank—until hell freezes over for all I care!"

For a second Kelsey thought he might storm out of the room. She almost wished he would. She'd like to eat her meals alone. But he lowered his blazing eyes to his plate and the tense moment passed.

She stared at the number on the pad. It was astonishing. How much would it cost to have a commercial kitchen built? How long would it take? Could it be completed in the same two months she was renovating the house, in time to meet her timetable for moving?

When he finished eating, Jared pushed back from the table cleared his plate and left the kitchen without saying another word. In a few moments Kelsey heard the rip of old wood on the porch and knew he'd started his afternoon's work.

Slowly she cleaned up from lunch, her mind occupied

with thoughts of the money Jared sent her every month. She hadn't known about it. And the number on the pad was huge, showing he must had increased the amount over the years.

Conscience money she called it.

Or support money as he said, for his wife.

The wife he'd conveniently forgotten about when she was in Dallas and he in California.

Kelsey went to call her aunt Ellie.

"Hello, Kelsey. I didn't expect you to call for another day or two. We've been baking up a storm. I miss having you around, though. How are things going there?"

Ellie's forthright manner was a comfort.

"Aunt Ellie, Jared's here," Kelsey blurted out, knowing that the real reason for her call was to get some help.

Jared was proving to be more than she could handle. She wouldn't last two months—she needed some backup.

"So that's it."

There was a lengthy silence on the other end then, "What are you doing about it?"

"He's offered to help me fix up the house."

"But?"

"But he won't agree to selling cattle to get money for building the commercial kitchen. He wants to keep the ranch going."

"And what does he think we can use for money? Your good looks?"

"He...um...put money in an account for me all along. He says I should use that."

"And you don't want to," Ellie guessed.

"No. Only there's a lot of money in the account. He said he won't take it back. It'd enable us to build a commercial kitchen completely state of the art all the way."

"That makes business sense. Once we're a smashing success, you can repay the man, if you want to. Take it, Kelsey. We need it. Don't let foolish pride stand in your way."

"Come stay with me," Kelsey said.

"Good grief, I guess Jared's still as charming as ever?" Ellie asked, immediately suspecting the reason for Kelsey's request.

"Devastating." Kelsey was honest.

Even knowing what she did about Jared, she was having trouble keeping away from him. She needed a no-nonsense chaperon.

"Well, it might be fun at that." Ellie chuckled softly. "I'll be there by dinner tomorrow. But, Kelsey, only on one condition."

"What's that?"

"Don't tell Jared before I arrive."

Kelsey had no trouble agreeing to that. He'd be furious when he found out what she'd done. Ellie was one of the few people in the family who still thought of and treated Jared as a young boy. She wasn't impressed by fame and fortune, or dark eyes that melted her heart. Or the smile that could break hearts.

Kelsey went back to work with a lighter heart. She'd be able to handle Jared with Aunt Ellie to back her up. And with that hurdle behind her, the rest would be easier.

Jared worked until late. When Kelsey started down

the stairs from taking a quick shower, he began climbing them. He paused halfway up when he saw her. She was fresh and cool. Her hair was still damp from her shower, and darker because of it, curling around her forehead, brushing her cheeks. She had put on a light sundress, because of the heat, and was barefoot.

She paused and stared down at him, her heart tripping once in its steady beat. He looked hot and sweaty and tired. And sexy as could be.

She tried a deep breath, but it caught in her throat and she couldn't look away. His dark eyes drew her into their depths and she stared back at him and feeling her body warm while flashes of memory seared her.

Jared broke contact and climbed the remaining steps in short order.

"I won't be here for dinner. I'm eating at the cafe in town, then going to meet with Jim. I saw you piled up the ranch records the other day. I'll take the most recent to review with him."

"Wouldn't you rather use the office?"

She hadn't meant to say it. She'd arranged things to suit herself. Not Jared. Why change now?

"Doesn't appear to be room for me there. I'll make do for now."

He brushed past her and went to his room, closing the door behind him.

Kelsey ignored the twinge of loneliness as she ate dinner alone, conscious of the empty place opposite her. She'd wanted this at lunch, but eating alone wasn't as much fun as sparring with Jarred.

She spent the evening sketching out different designs

for a commercial kitchen. She walked around the yard, again thinking the location beneath the old oak trees would be the best spot, close to the house yet not too close. In the shade, a nice setting.

Air conditioning was a must. She considered having that installed in the house before even starting on the kitchen. It'd make such a difference in getting the house ready. With the windfall for the kitchen, she had more to spend on fixing up the house.

She'd also made up her mind about the bank account. She'd use the money and pay Jared back every penny as soon as she was able. She felt a little awkward using it after her grand words to him before. But Ellie was right—it made good business sense.

Five

Kelsey awoke early the next morning, a feeling of anticipation filling her now that the decision was made. Today was the day she was going into town to talk to a contractor or two about the new kitchen. She was eager to get started. The sooner she completed it, the quicker she'd set up her business here at the ranch and begin expansion.

It was going to be challenging with both Ellie and herself here at Windhaven with the rest of the crew still in Dallas. She couldn't wait to move the entire operation to Windhaven.

Aunt Ellie would arrive this afternoon. At some point during the day Kelsey clean one of the bedrooms. She'd make sure Ellie didn't have to fend for herself when she arrived as Jared had.

She didn't want Jared to discover their aunt's visit ahead of time either. She'd have to clean the bedroom when he outside.

Dressed in a soft pink top and jeans for the ride, Kelsey enjoyed the brief coolness in the early morning. She was glad she rose early, before the hot, humid air sapped her energy, made work more of a chore than she would normally find. She hoped their riding tour wouldn't extend to the hot part of the day. She didn't know how the cowboys stood it day after day.

A quick glance from the window assured her that Jared returned home last night. Her heart curiously light, she descended the stairs to prepare breakfast, wondering how his discussions had gone with the ranch foreman.

She heard the shower from the kitchen and broke three more eggs into the bowl to include his breakfast. The phone rang. Pulling everything off the stove, she hurried to the office to answer.

Another item on her list—get extensions in other rooms in the house. Or figure out how to get cell service out here.

"Jared Martin."

The connection was static-filled.

"He's not available now. Can I have him call you back?"

"Peter Marshall, Tri-Color Pictures. Have him call me at the office. He has the number. It's important."

"I'll see he gets the message."

Kelsey gently replaced the receiver.

It must be someone from the studio, she mused as she returned to the kitchen. Calling about the next film? she wondered.

Would Jared have to leave earlier than he'd originally thought? Why didn't that possibility make her happier?

No sooner had she put the things back on the stove than the phone rang again. Half tempted to let it ring, she turned off the burners and hurried back to the office. She definitely needed a phone for the kitchen.

"Hello?"

"Jared, please."

The voice was low, sultry, seductive. And definitely feminine.

"He can't come to the phone right now. May I take a message?"

Who was this?

"Is he there?"

"Yes, he's here, but he's unavailable right now."

"Who are you?"

The voice on the other end was decidedly not from Texas.

For one brief second Kelsey toyed with the idea of claiming to be his wife. Would that set this woman back on her heels?

She sighed softly. No way of finding out. She wouldn't claim it, not knowing what Jared would do if he heard about it.

"His cousin," was all Kelsey said.

"Where's Jared?"

"He's in the shower, if you must know."

Kelsey listened intently to her voice. Was she the one from that fateful morning? There was something familiar about it, but she didn't think the voice was the same. Would she even recognize it after all this time?

"Then I'll hold on until he's through. Go tell him Pamela Hughes is waiting to talk to him."

Conscious of the clock ticking, Kelsey raced up the stairs, pounding on the bathroom door.

It opened and Jared stared at her in surprise. A towel was knotted around his waist. His hair was still damp and tousled. Shaving-cream lathered his cheeks. His chest was broad and tanned, filling Kelsey's vision. She stopped short.

And aware of him as never before.

"Is something wrong?" he asked.

Kelsey swallowed hard. The crisp hair on his chest held her attention. She longed to run her fingers over his skin, tangling gently with the hair, feeling his muscles ripple and move beneath her touch. Awareness tingled through her body. She had forgotten how sexy he looked. How she longed to touch him—

"Kelsey?" He stood patiently in the doorway, not at all bothered by his attire or her hungry gaze.

"There's a phone call for you. Pamela Hughes. She said to let you know she's holding."

Kelsey dragged her eyes up to meet his, color staining her cheeks.

"Pamela? What does she want?" he said, more to himself than to her.

"To talk to you, I presume. She's holding," Kelsey said sharply, annoyed that Jared had seen her interest.

Jared's gaze sharpened as he took in Kelsey's flushed face. He smiled sardonically.

"Of course she does. She was my leading lady in the last two films and we're doing the next one together. Quite a beautiful woman and talented to boot."

Kelsey felt the sting of jealousy as she turned away and forced herself to walk calmly down the hall. She was proud of her casual,

"Well, the phone is on the desk in the office. I'm going back to the kitchen."

He'd never called her beautiful, she thought, as she walked down the stairs. She'd barely reached the bottom when Jared hurried by her, wiping the shaving-cream from his face with a towel, the other still around his waist.

Kelsey ached to know why he'd received two calls in such a short time. Was there an emergency that required his presence? Would he leave before the two months were up? How much longer would he stay at Windhaven?

Beyond that, she had no interest in what he did with his life, what his future plans were. Plans that obviously didn't include her.

She finished her breakfast by the time Jared joined her in the kitchen. Placing his food before him without speaking, she turned to wash her dish. Though raging with curiosity, she refrained from asking about the calls, telling him only that Peter Marshall had also called.

She had other issues—like how to tell him that she was planning to use the money he'd put in the bank account to build her commercial kitchen after all.

Would he gloat that he'd gotten his way? Make some snide comment about her not being able to manage without him for all her fine talk?

"Jim and I'll be back in plenty of time for me to help finish stripping the dining-room today," he said casually, as he finished his breakfast..

"Actually, I'm going into Willowby this morning," she began, her eyes firmly on the last dish she was washing. "To talk to a builder about my kitchen."

"That pattern won't wash off, Kelsey, no matter how much you try," Jared said, amused.

She flushed and rinsed the plate, putting it on the rack to drain.

"Who are you going to see?" he asked.

"I don't know. I thought I'd ask around. Get a recommendation."

"I'll go with you when you go. We'll ask Jim this morning. He'll know who's good. But he's planning our ride and I don't want to back out of that."

"You go."

"I told him we'd both go."

She stood in indecision. She'd been interested in seeing more of the ranch that morning. And it had been ages since she'd ridden a horse. She'd loved it when younger.

"But in light of everything going on—"

"We won't be gone that long. Then we can go to town. You do have half ownership of this ranch, don't you want to see it all?"

She nodded. "Okay, but with the ride and the trip to town, I doubt we'll get much wallpaper stripping done."

"One day won't throw off the schedule," he commented.

It was a short walk to the barn. Far enough from the house so the tearoom wouldn't interfere with ranch operations, yet close enough tourists could get a glimpse of ranching operations.

Jim had three horses saddled and ready when Kelsey and Jared arrived. Jared introduced Kelsey to the foreman and before long they were riding toward the cattle visible from the house.

Jim talked about acreage and expected sales prices per

pound. Kelsey listened feeling totally lost sometimes, but if they were going to keep the ranch running, she needed to know enough to make decisions—thus taking away the need for Jared to come back anytime there was a problem.

They rode for more than an hour.

Kelsey had a much better idea of how large the ranch was. Once again her imagination took flight and at one point she saw no sign of man. This was what the land looked like when her ancestors settled. She reined in her horse and gazed around her.

Jared stopped. "What?" he asked.

She took a deep breath and smiled.

"I was imagining I was coming here for the first time—back in the 1800s when the ranch first started. This is how it looked and it still doesn't have a lot of man-made intrusions."

Jared looked around, then back at Jim. "Is all this part of the original ranch?"

Jim nodded. "The land on the far side of the house was acquired in the early 1900s as I heard. But this was the first part."

"Are any of the cattle descended from that first herd?" Kelsey asked.

Jim shook his head. "No, Henry improved the herd over the years. But as I heard, he pretty much started fresh. The depression hit this area hard back in the 1930s. His father did the best he could, but times were tough. They sold off most of the herd to keep a roof over their head."

They started up again. Kelsey tried to pay attention, but as the morning progressed she became impatient.

It was fun to ride again, but time was ticking by and she wanted to see if she could hire a contractor to start on the kitchen. If this was to be her home in the future, she'd have plenty of time to explore and learn more.

"Should we be heading back?" she asked a half-hour later.

"Already on our way," Jim said. "We've been making a wide sweep. We'll be back in twenty minutes or less."

When they returned to the barn, Kelsey thanked the foreman for the information. She told him she'd like to ride out with the cowboys one day, but had to get things organized at the house first.

She turned to Jared. "I'm going to clean up and head for town. You're on your own for lunch."

"I told you I'd go in with you. We'll take the bike."

"I have a perfectly good car. I don't need to ride on that donor-mobile of yours."

He grinned at her. "You'll love it. I'll be ready to go by the time you are."

Kelsey wanted to protest, but the look of expectancy on Jared's face made her hold her tongue. She refused to give him the satisfaction of arguing—especially in front of Jim.

Instead she nodded abruptly and left before she said or did something outrageous.

The sun was already high in the sky, the day going to be another scorcher.

She was glad he insisted on going with her. He'd obviously be better at construction talk with his background.

She understood cooking and marketing and distribution. But building kitchens was beyond her. She had an idea of what she wanted. She hoped Jared could get the best deal.

As she stepped onto the porch, she paused to study what had already been accomplished.

Much of it had been repaired, boards replaced, others tightened. It looked ready for paint. She scanned the front of the house. She noted all the work needing to be done on the shutters and window frames.

How had Uncle Henry let it go so badly?

He'd been old, very old. Still, it was a shame.

Hurrying inside, Kelsey headed straight for the shower. She smelled of horse and didn't want that to be the first impression to give to the people in town.

Once dressed Kelsey went back downstairs, looking for Jared. She wore tailored trousers and a loose-fitting top. Shorts were fine around the house, but for a business meeting in town they weren't quite the thing. And riding on Jared's motorcycle precluded wearing a dress.

He sat on the motorcycle waiting for her. His navy T-shirt displayed his muscular shoulders and chest and emphasized his tight stomach and narrow waist. His dark hair gleamed in the sunlight still slightly damp from his shower.

Some of that light danced in the depths of his brown eyes when he watched Kelsey walk reluctantly down the steps.

She eyed the motorcycle with a certain amount of trepidation. She'd never ridden on one before. Maybe she should insist on her car.

Without a word Jared kick started it. Its roar filled the morning air, throaty and powerful. Birds squawked at the intrusion on their peaceful day and some fluttered out of the nearby trees.

"Come on, Kel, we don't have all day."

Jared patted the seat behind him, his eyes challenging her.

Too late Kelsey realized how they would have to travel. She'd be pressed right up against him, holding on to him to keep her balance. Her body would be flush against his for the entire ride.

Her heart began pounding against her chest. She couldn't do it. It was too much.

"I..." She started to protest, to tell him she'd changed her mind, that she'd take her car after all.

"Come on. I've got work to do here, too. The quicker we leave the sooner we'll be back." Jared's tone certainly didn't sound seductive.

She hesitated only a moment, then moved to mount the machine. Throwing her leg over, she sat gingerly on the padded seat. Its structure prevented her from maintaining any distance from Jared. She slipped right up against him.

He handed her a helmet. "Wear this."

"It's yours. What will you wear?"

"When we're in town, I'll get another one. For this ride, you wear the helmet."

She put it on, fastening the strap beneath her chin. Pulling down the face plate, she was pleased she could see as well as without a helmet.

"Put your arms around me and hold on. Lean with

91

me when I lean. Relax, Kelsey. I haven't wrecked one of these yet."

Kelsey tentatively put her hands on his waist, holding lightly, feeling the warmth of his muscles beneath her. His hands clamped on hers and brought them around until she clasped her own hands. Her arms held him and her breasts were pressed into the strong muscles of his back.

She could hardly breathe.

"Hold on tight. We'll be going fast and the road's bumpy until we hit the main highway."

Kelsey felt a shock of awareness touching him. She longed to let her hands roam over his body, revel in his strength, discover the changes the years had brought. She moved her fingers slightly.

"And keep your hands where they are. If they drop, I may break my perfect record," Jared growled as he revved the motor.

Maybe this was a mistake, Jared thought as they took off. How would he stand her pressing against him for the duration of the trip into town?

Kelsey felt the vibration of the motorcycle beneath her engulfing her. When Jared started off, she clutched tightly, leaning against him as he'd instructed and praying they'd make it home alive.

In only seconds she realized it was like flying! The air streamed by her, warm and soft in the morning sun. The power of the machine gave her confidence and Jared's handling of the bike on the rough driveway was wonderful.

She watched the ground dash by at an alarming rate, then lifted her eyes to look around. It was amazing—no wonder he loved riding a motorcycle. Without the metal of a car surrounding her, she felt alive.

"This is super!" she said near his ear as a smile of delight broke across her face. "Do you drive this all the time?"

How could she have lived her twenty-seven years and never ridden a motorcycle before?

"Yes, but maybe not for the reason you think." His voice was tossed back by the blowing wind.

"What reason?" she asked, enchanted with the freedom the bike gave, the feeling of floating on air, flying. It was glorious!

"To outrun the devil that plagues me," was his bleak reply.

Kelsey was shocked. Seconds later she hardened her heart. He ought to experience devils. She'd had enough heartache to last five lifetimes because of him.

She was oddly satisfied that he hadn't got off Scot-free himself.

A sweeping curve came up fast. Jared leaned to the right, the bike leaning over as it smoothly took the turn. Kelsey, mindful of his instructions, leaned with him, feeling in tune with his body, moving as he did.

The road rushing by was so close that she thought she could trail her fingers down and touch it. Suddenly she was afraid.

"We'd be badly hurt if we crashed, wouldn't we?" she asked.

"Yes. But I don't crash." Jared's reply was confident, simply stated.

Kelsey believed him. She'd trust her life to Jared Martin.

And that surprised her.

They'd asked Jim during the ride on the best contractors to contact and she'd called from the house to make sure he could see them.

She also wanted to learn more about Jared's opinion of Windhaven as a self-sufficient ranch. If she learned enough, Jared wouldn't have to visit. She'd be able to oversee things and make sure he got his share of any proceeds.

They soon reached the main road. Jared increased speed and she ducked behind him, resting her head against his broad shoulders, watching the scenery whiz by as they headed for Willowby.

They stopped for lunch at the town's main café, then spent the early afternoon with the builder they selected, Sam Clark, going over the requirements, drafting rough plans.

He told them he'd get back to them with rough drawings and estimates by the first of the week, after he'd had a chance to study the chosen site.

Next they went shopping for paint and wallpaper. Jared arranged for everything to be delivered the next day. Kelsey was surprised at how smoothly the afternoon went, how similar their tastes were. It was easy to agree to each of the choices, since they both liked the same patterns and colors.

The ride home was sweet. Kelsey loved the feeling of soaring across the ground, zipping past cars, watching the landscape sweep by, leaning into the turns, the wind flowing through the helmet, the sunlight on her arms. It was glorious.

Would she ever have another opportunity?

Probably not.

She tightened her grip a little, trying to hold on to the moment. Had things been different she'd do this again. But nothing would ever change their past.

When he drew near the barn, he slowed and stopped. Kelsey looked around, puzzled.

"Why did we stop here?"

"I wanted to look at the house from a distance, see it all. Try to envisage how it'll look after it's painted."

They'd decided on white paint for the siding, dark green for the shutters and trim. Kelsey peered over his shoulder, also trying to envision what it would look like when finished. It wasn't much now, merely a tired old building in disrepair.

It'd look charming when the renovations were finished. The trees surrounding it gave it a settled, established look. The branches surrounding the house softened the harsh lines. When repaired and painted, flower gardens planted, it'd be perfect.

"Do we need a new roof?" she asked, frowning. The roof looked awful now that she saw the whole house in one glance. How much more would that cost?

"May need repairs. I didn't notice any water damage when I walked through the house, but it looks pretty old."

"It's going to look nice, isn't it?" she said softly, smiling in anticipation.

It was going to be perfect for Grandma's.

And for a family, she thought unexpectedly.

"Yes."

He remained silent for a moment, then spoke carefully.

"Kelsey, I have to be in Los Angeles in a couple of weeks. The studio wants me there for the opening night of my latest film. And a pre-production planning meeting for the next picture. I want you to go with me."

She stiffened. Before she pulled away, however, Jared's hand clamped over hers, keeping her in place.

"No," she said.

Tiny currents of electricity seemed to shoot up her arms from his touch. Her heart pounded. She swallowed hard, tried to pull back, to put some distance between them.

"Don't say no now. Think on it at least. I want you to go with me."

"Why?"

He shrugged. "To meet some people. Take a break from this place. By that time, we'll both relish a break. When was the last time you were in LA?"

"Ages ago. I don't want to go. I don't need to think about it."

"Do it anyway, that's all I ask right now," he said again.

She drew in a deep breath. "All right," she said reluctantly, wondering if she'd ever be able to stop thinking about it.

But time wasn't going to change her mind.

Why did he want her to go? Why would he want her at the opening night of one of his films? She remembered the flashing photographers, the crowds lining the entry.

"When's the opening?" she asked.

"The premier will be in Los Angeles in a couple of weeks. They want me there for the publicity."

"I don't want to go."

She hadn't liked the one she'd participated once when she and Jared had first been married. It was awful. The crush of people, the paparazzi with their cameras flashing incessantly. Obnoxious reporters asking personal questions, constantly making snide insinuations.

She didn't need any of that. Jared was welcome to it.

"I'm asking nicely," he said.

She was silent, struck by his request.

He'd never asked before. In the past he'd always assumed she'd attend.

He put the motorcycle in gear and in only moments they pulled up in front of the house.

"We won't get much work done today," he said as Kelsey got off. Swinging his leg over, he swiveled and remained seated on the bike, taking off his new helmet while watching her through his dark glasses.

"We accomplished a lot in town. That's a kind of work. And tomorrow we can finish stripping the dining room," she said nervously, standing near him as if unable to leave, twisting her helmet around and around.

"Kelsey."

He reached out and took the helmet, hooking it on the handlebars and took her hand in his, his thumb making lazy circles against her wrist.

After a moment Kelsey snatched back her hand, shaking her head and backing away.

"Don't, Jared, just don't."

Turning, she fled into the house.

After donning shorts and a cool top, Kelsey went to clean the bedroom beyond Jared's for Aunt Ellie's use. It was musty and dank. She threw open the windows, pausing for a moment when she saw Jared marking off the plot for the new kitchen. She watched for a long moment, her heart aching, vague longings rising up and threatening to overpower her.

Resolutely turning her back on him, she set to work.

Ellie Langford arrived at Windhaven Ranch shortly before dinner. Kelsey, Jared and Billy were sanding the porch in preparation for painting when Ellie's car came down the drive. Jared paused and watched with curiosity as the car approached.

Kelsey flicked a nervous glance first at the car, then at Jared, and licked suddenly dry lips.

She should have told him. Prepared him. Anxiously she watched for his reaction.

He caught her staring at him. His eyes narrowed slightly, then his gaze moved back to the car, suspicion dawning.

"You expecting company?" he asked as it drove up and parked right in front of the house, near his bike.

Ellie thrust open the door and climbed out, a tall woman with iron-gray hair. Her eyes met Kelsey's and moved on to meet Jared's surprised look.

"Hello, you two. Come help me with my bags."

She gave them a cheery wave and went to open the trunk.

"Ellie," Jared said. His gaze swinging immediately to Kelsey. "What's she doing here?"

Kelsey jumped up and hurried to the car, giving her aunt a big hug then reaching for a suitcase. She expected he'd be angry. She should have told him.

"Hello, Aunt Ellie."

Jared's tone was neutral as he walked slowly to greet her, leaning over to give her a light peck on her cheek.

"Surprised to see me?" Ellie asked, not waiting for the answer.

She reached into the trunk for a small bag.

"A bit. Kelsey didn't tell me you were coming. Staying long?"

He looked at her luggage, the stacks of boxes in the back of the car.

"As long as it takes," was the vague answer.

"Your room's made up, Aunt Ellie. Did you bring packaging boxes and papers? We can start work here on a limited basis with the existing kitchen. The guy from the health department will come out next week to inspect the kitchen. In the meantime we'll have enough to experiment with new cookies at least."

Kelsey tried to keep her aunt between herself and Jared. He looked annoyed.

"Of course," was the placid reply. "Show me my room. My, my, Henry sure let this place go to ruin," Ellie said as she gazed around.

She ignored the tension between her two young relatives, a small smile tugging the edges of her mouth, and headed for the front door, nodding to Billy in passing.

Kelsey led the way upstairs, chatting with her aunt,

telling her what they'd done already, what the plans were for the renovation. She touched lightly on the plans for the commercial kitchen.

Jared still hadn't made any comment about her using the money. But she suspected he would. And probably bring it up at the most inopportune time.

He followed carrying two suitcases, dumping them in Ellie's room with a thump. He turned and scanned the room, noting how clean it was. Leaving, he paused in the doorway.

"Coming, Kelsey? I'm sure Aunt Ellie wants to get settled in."

His voice was like silk. Dark, dangerous silk. He glared at Kelsey, daring her to refuse.

Kelsey hesitated, but received no support from Ellie, no request to stay and help her unpack. That lady merely watched to see what Kelsey did.

Finally she raised her chin and stepped from the room, closing the door behind her.

"What is Ellie doing here?" he asked, teeth gritted, as they walked down the hall toward the stairs. "And why didn't you tell me she was coming?"

Kelsey's heartbeat sped up as she stared up into his angry face.

"It didn't come up," she said, her eyes caught by his.

"That's not something that has to come up—you out and out tell a person. How long have you known?"

"Since yesterday."

"And why is she here?"

"Because she's my partner and needs to see what we're doing."

"You're lying, Kelsey. She's here for protection. A chaperone if you will. What are you afraid of? Me? Or yourself?"

"Don't be ridiculous."

"I'm not being ridiculous. You respond to me every time I kiss you—and I know you hate responding. Do you want a sample?"

He leaned against her, his free hand capturing her jaw gently as his mouth captured hers.

Despite her best efforts Kelsey began to respond, annoyed with her traitorous body even as she felt the pull of desire from his touch.

And he knew it, exactly as he'd said.

He pulled back in triumph. His eyes glittered down at her as his smug, sardonic smile taunted her. "See what I mean?"

"Go away, Jared. Get out of here! I won't be used by you," she spat out at him, her free hand wiping her mouth as if to erase the touch of him, the feel of him, the very taste of him. As if she wanted to.

"Kelsey, I told you I'm staying two months to work on renovating this place. At the end, I want my wife back. Be warned, I always get what I want."

His voice was deadly serious.

"Not this time," she said with as much bravado as she could muster.

Her heart was beating so fast, she felt as if she'd run a long race. Breathing was difficult. He was so close, so tantalizing, so sexy.

"Always! Remember that!"

He stormed away and ran down the stairs.

Kelsey leaned against the wall, afraid that her knees would give way. She crossed her arms over her chest as she heard the roar of the motorcycle, listened until it faded in the distance.

He was gone.

Wasn't it what she wanted?

Why wasn't she happier?

Why was there a throbbing ache in her heart?

Six

Kelsey tossed and turned that night, unable to sleep. Jared didn't return for supper and the meal seemed somehow flat with only Ellie. Before coming to Windhaven, Kelsey spent endless hours discussing business with her aunt—making plans, discussing sales strategies, reviewing where they stood all seemed so compelling before.

Tonight Kelsey listened in vain for the roar of the motorcycle, longed for Jared's disturbing presence.

Ellie told Kelsey she'd handed over the responsibility for the baking and distribution of the cookies from Dallas to one of their part-time assistants, giving her the extra hours she needed to stay on top of things.

She'd brought boxes and packaging papers with her and planned to get as much work done at Windhaven as possible.

"First step, get this kitchen certified for commercial use," she said.

"The man'll be here this week," Kelsey murmured.

"You've had a lot on your mind. I'll call in the morning to see if he'll come out any earlier," Ellie said. "Is there a local wholesaler where we can get ingredients?"

Kelsey tried to pay attention to her aunt's enthusiastic planning, but her attention kept wandering. Where was Jared?

"Kelsey?"

She looked at her aunt. "What?"

"I asked about wholesale supplies."

"I talked with the manager of the Save Well in town, he'll order for us until we get a regular supplier who can deliver."

The evening had seemed endless.

Kelsey rolled over in her bed and peered at her clock. She gazed dry-eyed in to the dark, wondering where Jared was and when he'd return.

She hoped he hadn't had an accident with that motorcycle.

It'd have been better if he hadn't come at all. Why couldn't he sell her his half of the ranch? She'd sell the cattle and lease out the range to raise money. She'd be able to pay his share easily enough.

All she needed was the home and surrounding acres. If he was serious about keeping his half, however, she didn't stand a chance of changing his mind.

She remembered how stubborn he was once he got an idea in his head.

She sat up, straining to listen in the darkness. In the distance she heard the drone of the motorcycle. Then it got quiet. Was he staying at the cowboys' bunkhouse?

No, it sounded like it was coming closer, but muffled somehow.

She rose and ran to the window, gazing out into the dark night. The stars were brilliant in the black dome, no moon to dim their sparkle. She saw the single headlight of the motorcycle as it passed the barn and headed for the house.

He muffled the engine. That was why she hadn't heard him come home the other nights. For a moment she was struck by his sensitivity to the noise if people were trying to sleep.

She watched him through the window, seeing only his shadow and silhouette in the black night.

Sadly she acknowledged she'd loved him all her life and, despite what had happened, that hadn't changed.

She went back to bed when he stepped on the porch, tears flooding her eyes.

A part of her had died that long-ago day in London. She'd never been the same since.

But her love for Jared hadn't ended, much as she wished it would.

She drew up the sheet, longing for the escape of sleep.

Kelsey was not at all rested when she awoke at dawn. Knowing further sleep was impossible, she rose and quickly dressed. She'd get an early start on the dining room, do what she could to hasten this renovation project. Stay so busy she didn't have time to dwell on anything.

Early as she was, Aunt Ellie was already in the kitchen when Kelsey entered.

"What are you doing up so early?" she asked, giving her aunt a kiss on the cheek.

She went to the coffee maker and poured herself a cup.

"I wanted to get an early start. Lots to do today and

if it stays this hot, I want to be in town in air-conditioned buildings as soon as I can. Why Henry didn't air condition this place is beyond me."

Kelsey laughed. "I know. That's going to be the first thing I do is get this place air conditioned."

"We'll need it if we bake at all in this kitchen. What are you planning for the commercial kitchen?"

Kelsey reviewed her plans for the new kitchen, showing Ellie the spot she'd chosen.

"But so far, I've only talked with one contractor. I liked the man. He told me he'd have preliminary drawings for us next week. In the meantime, we've been working on the renovation for the tearoom."

"Tell me more about what you envision when you move our operations here. Now that I see it, I'm not sure it's going to work."

"It'll be perfect when fixed up. I visited once when I was about ten. It was in much better condition then. I want to make it shine. It'll be an example of old ranches whose histories go back to the 1800s and highlight nostalgia. Don't you think it'll help expand Grandma's Cookies? I was thinking a YouTube video of the tearoom, then panning out to the barn, cattle in the distance. People will be able to envision Grandma here in this old ranch house."

Ellie drew out a chair and pulled a small notebook from her large apron pocket. "Okay, that's one aspect. Fix up the house. Have the website focus on the new location. What else will we need to do to bring about this miracle?"

They were still making the list when Jared entered

some time later. Kelsey looked up, and was unable to look away.

He looked tired. He hadn't shaved and the darkness along his jaw intrigued her. What would his stubble feel like against her fingertips? It had been so long.

"Good morning." His voice was low, soft, seductive.

For a moment Kelsey forgot Aunt Ellie, forgot Windhaven Ranch, forgot the heartbreak of the past.

She saw only Jared, heard only his soft velvet tone that always touched her.

"You're another who's up early, boy. Want breakfast?" Ellie noticed nothing, slapping shut the notebook and rising. "Eggs all right with you? Kelsey?"

Kelsey blinked and looked away, puzzled. What had Ellie asked?

"Eggs are fine, Aunt Ellie. Kelsey likes hers scrambled."

Jared pulled out the chair beside Kelsey and sat down, his eyes never leaving her.

When she moved to rise, he reached out and caught her wrist, tugging gently so that she sat back in her chair.

"What?" she said, pulling her arm away.

"Stay and talk."

His voice was low, for her ears only.

"About what?"

"Are you coming with me to Los Angeles?"

"When are you going to LA, Jared?" Aunt Ellie asked from the stove. There was nothing wrong with her hearing.

"In a couple of weeks. For a few days."

"Great. Kelsey, you should go with him. I'll watch

things here and you can follow up on Markham's request to meet with him face to face. That'd be perfect."

She broke several eggs in the bowl and whipped them vigorously.

"Markham?" Jared asked.

"Business. But I don't need to go there for that—I can call him," Kelsey said to her aunt.

She hadn't even thought about the Markham account. It'd give her a business reason to go to California. She didn't want to give the wrong impression if she decided to go to LA.

"Business negotiations always go better face to face," Ellie said.

Jared smiled at Kelsey's dilemma.

"All right, I'll go," she said, irritated.

So far Aunt Ellie presence hadn't helped the way Kelsey thought it would.

Even after her arrival, Jared had kissed her again.

And now she was committed to going to LA with the man.

Ellie was supposed to protect her against his charms, not help him.

When breakfast was finished, Jared left the women and headed for the dining room and the work that remained.

"I'll go with you into town to get the supplies," Kelsey said as she washed the dishes.

"No need. I'm perfectly capable of doing that myself. I have been to Willowby before, you know. You help Jared clean this place up," Ellie responded, drying the plates and replacing in the cupboard.

Kelsey looked at her, puzzled by the odd tone in her voice.

"Aunt Ellie, what are you up to?"

"Trying to get this business going. Why's Jared here?"

"To protect his inheritance."

"I don't think so. He could do that with lawyers," Ellie said.

"Well, he wanted to sell the ranch outright, but I convinced him to give me a chance to use the house. Now he's talking about keeping the ranch going, making it pay."

Ellie was silent as she put away the last of the dishes and silverware, deep in thought.

"I never figured him for a cowboy. But he was raised in Texas. He's a descendant of old Abraham. What happened four years ago, Kelsey? You never told me, only that the marriage was over and you never wanted to see him again. And you've never brought it up in all the time since then," Ellie asked gently, turning to look at her niece.

Kelsey stared out of the window, her eyes blind to the view bright in the morning sun. She saw instead Jared's shocked face in bed that morning, saw that woman and her skimpy nightclothes.

"I went to see him, to surprise him when he was in London, and found him with another woman."

Her voice was as dead as she felt inside. Even after all this time, it still hurt.

"And what did Jared say about it?" Ellie asked calmly.

Kelsey frowned and turned to her aunt. "Nothing. I ran. I didn't stay to discuss the situation."

"But afterwards?"

Kelsey dried her hands and carefully hung the towel

on the hook.

"I've never discussed it with him. That part of my life is over."

"You need to ask him his side of what happened. Even if it confirms everything, give him a chance to explain why it happened," Ellie said gently.

"Why, so he can tell me how inadequate I was? How as a wife I couldn't hold my husband? How naive and childish compared to his glamorous movie stars? No, thanks, Aunt Ellie. I know all I need to know."

Recognizing a brick wall when she saw it, Ellie shrugged. "I think you're making a mistake. The one thing I've learned over the years is people have to learn some things through adversity."

"So what doesn't kill us, makes us stronger," Kelsey said.

Ellie nodded. "I've made a list for the market, you go on and let's get this place fixed up."

Kelsey passed the office on her way to the dining room and saw Jared sitting at her desk, reviewing some papers.

"What are you doing?" she asked from the doorway.

He glanced up and then back down to the papers.

"Checking out the most recent sales report Uncle Henry had. I want to discuss this with Jim and some other ranchers in the area. I'm not sure Henry got the best deal."

"Why are you doing this in my office?"

Jared looked up at that, raising one eyebrow. "Your office? We inherited this place share and share alike, sweetheart. It's our office."

"I put the stuff I thought you'd need by the door."

"I saw it. Now I have it here where I can read it. I'll find a place to file what I want to keep." Jared leaned back in the chair, putting his feet on the desk.

"Find someplace else."

"This place suits me fine."

"I don't want you here."

He was taking over. His very presence filled the office. It wouldn't be big enough for the two of them to work in. Kelsey recognized the fact even if Jared didn't.

"Tough, Kel. I'm here and I'm staying. There's plenty of room. We'll bring in another desk." His gaze was level, his tone calm but definite. He was not moving.

"I need a large desk. I have a computer coming and files. You're only here for another few weeks."

She sat down in the chair against the wall and glared at him.

Jared's lips twitched and his eyes danced in sudden amusement, which only served to antagonize Kelsey.

"What are you playing at now? Cattle rancher—what do you know about that anyway?"

"Not much, I admit. But I can learn. I have a good business background. I took courses at the university and I worked with the associate producer of the last two pictures I starred in. I know about budgets and revenue versus expenses. What I don't know about cattle I'll learn."

"Sell me your share," she said again.

"Not a chance."

Kelsey was so annoyed she could spit! He could do his paperwork elsewhere. He was only dabbling in this. Once his two months were up, he'd be leaving to star in another film. He'd be gone for months and then who'd watch the ranch?

His life was elsewhere. Why couldn't he go back to it and leave her in peace?

"Come here and let me show you some of the figures."

He sat up and moved his gaze back to the page before him, pencil in hand.

Reluctantly she rose and moved to stand near the desk, craning her neck trying to read the numbers.

"Come around here. I'm not going to bite you—delectable as the thought may be," he teased her.

"No."

He reached out and captured her hand, pulling her around the side of the desk to stand beside his chair. When he released her Kelsey snatched back her hand, putting it behind her.

"No touching, that's part of the truce," she said.

"And you need to remember another part of the truce—that we're to get along. You're as prickly as a porcupine."

"You're deliberately annoying me."

"Not true."

He stared at her until she dropped her gaze to stare at the sheet of paper in front of him, refusing to look at him again.

"We have an arbitrator now, if we have a truce dispute," he said whimsically.

"But not an impartial one," Kelsey muttered, trying to focus on the numbers listed on the paper, her body more attuned to the man beside her.

"Even you admit she favors you?" he asked.

"I don't think she favors me. She wants you to explain to me what happened that day. She's on your side," she blurted out, not knowing she was going to say that, bewildered that her ally turned on her like that.

She'd brought Aunt Ellie here for protection, not to advocate Jared's position.

Jared instantly went still, his eyes on her.

When the moments stretched out, he asked softly, "Do you want me to explain?"

She shook her head, her eyes refusing to meet his.

"I know what I saw. I was there, remember?"

With a small sound suspiciously like a sob, Kelsey darted around the desk and out of the front door, the screen banging sharply behind her.

Walking quickly, she headed for the trees, seeking shadows, whatever coolness to be found. She sank down on the grass, leaning against one of the old oak trees, her arms crossed over her chest as if trying to hold in the ache, her eyes filled with tears she wanted to end. It was old news. The hurt should have faded by now.

A twig snapped nearby and she turned. Jared was standing next to her, his face in the shadow. Slowly he sank down beside her and turned to lean against the same trunk as Kelsey.

"Go away," she said, dashing the tears from her cheek.

"Maybe Aunt Ellie's right. It's long past time when we should have talked about that day."

"I don't want to hear it."

She couldn't bear to have him tell her how he'd

needed more than he had in their marriage—and found it with the women he worked with.

"I meant my wedding vows when I said them, Kelsey. I thought we'd have a marriage for all time. Only I wasn't really thinking about you when we married, just me. I wanted you—like always. I didn't consider what the marriage would be like for you with me gone so much. I was so caught up in the new contract I'd just received, the opportunities for bigger parts in bigger pictures. I didn't realize you'd feel neglected."

She closed her eyes. Nothing she'd say would stop him. She'd have to listen to the end and hope she didn't break down.

"I should have taken you with me to Europe. But I was full of my new status and you were young. I didn't want to take you so far from your family to fend for yourself in a foreign country while I was working."

Young, naive and so much in love as to be embarrassing to her sophisticated husband. Kelsey remembered how she'd been. And how much she'd missed him when he'd left.

"I don't need this, Jared. It's over and done with. No excuse will change the past."

"I'm not excusing anything, blast it. Nothing happened!"

She turned to look at him, rising up on her knees, anger giving her strength.

"You don't have to tell me how young I was, how inadequate I was for the great Jared Martin. Do you think I don't already know that?"

"What are you talking about? It wasn't that at all!"

She put her hands over her ears. "I don't want to hear any more!" she shouted.

He moved like lightning to face her, to drag her hands from her head and hold her wrists in his tight fists.

"You can bloody well listen. I didn't sleep with Sally. What you saw wasn't what it seemed. It's the honest truth. I don't want another woman in my life, Kelsey, only you!"

"Until the next party," she shot back, struggling to free herself.

"No!"

"I know what I saw!"

"You know nothing at all!"

His temper flared and he pulled her into his arms, his mouth descending on hers in a hard kiss. The scratchy stubble scraped her chin as his arms held her. His lips were hot against hers and Kelsey felt desire flood every cell.

The kiss went on and on. Kelsey couldn't help her response. Deep within her heat blossomed and built, a longing as old as time growing as her hands clutched his shoulders, moved to tangle in his thick, dark hair. His heart pounded heavily against her breast and Kelsey's heart matched it beat for beat.

She felt disoriented when he pushed her away, his dark eyes glittered, his mouth red and swollen from the kiss—as hers probably was. Slowly she moistened her lips with the tip of her tongue, warily staring back at him. She was afraid to move, even to breathe, lest she provoke him again.

Her breath mingled with his, blowing lightly across her cheeks, his cheeks, cooling the heat that had exploded between them.

"I'm going to work on the dining room," Jared said, anger still evident.

He rose with one lithe movement and turned to walk towards the house.

As if he hadn't turned Kelsey's world upside-down.

Again.

She watched him go, her heart rate gradually slowing, her breathing returning to normal. The world stopped whirling around her and settled down.

Kelsey went inside half an hour later when she saw Aunt Ellie leave. Conscious that she was alone with Jared, Kelsey hesitated only a moment before lifting her chin and marching into the dining room.

She refused to cower away from him because of their past. She had a right to be there, too.

He'd accomplished a lot in the short time he'd been working. She fell to the task with a will and they worked silently together. Almost compatibly, Kelsey thought, flicking a glance over at Jared from time to time.

The paint and wallpaper arrived. Jared and the deliveryman stacked the containers and rolls in the living room. Kelsey continued working while he dealt with the delivery. After that neither paused in the task until Ellie returned.

Kelsey left without a word to go help her aunt unload her car.

"Finished."

Jared came into the kitchen and pulled out a chair, sprawling down in it as he glanced at Kelsey and Ellie, flexing his hands tiredly.

"If you ever want to strip the new paper you're

planning to put up, count me out. I never want to strip another piece of wallpaper in my life."

He rotated his shoulders to ease the tension, flexing his hands again.

"It's awful, isn't it?" Kelsey murmured, pouring a tall glass of lemonade for each of them.

She placed Jared's before him, careful to avoid touching him, avoid looking at him.

As she sipped the tart liquid, she surreptitiously studied Jared, her mind reliving their kiss. Why was she still affected by him?

Jared saw her staring and reached over to cup her chin in his warm hand, his thumb brushing lightly over her lips in an erotic touch.

"Are you okay?" His voice was low, meant only for her ears.

Eyes wide, deep pools of blue, Kelsey shook her head slightly, not enough to dislodge his hand, only to respond. She held her breath, feeling the warmth from his fingers transfer to her, the heat rise in her cheeks, rise in her body, the pulse of power from Jared's fingers to the very soul of her being. Why couldn't things be different?

"I'm sorry."

His eyes held hers and time stood still.

For a long moment she thought he meant something else, something more than breaking their truce yet again. Maybe he also included that day in London so long ago.

How she wished he meant it.

"Kiss and make friends, that's what my mother always said." Ellie stood nearby, beaming from ear to ear.

Jared smiled slightly and rose, bent over Kelsey to

brush his lips lightly against hers, totally unconcerned that Ellie was watching.

"Friends?" he said softly, his dark eyes looking deep into hers.

"Truce, anyway," she replied, afraid of the roiling emotions he caused, afraid that she would blurt out how much she loved him despite everything.

Afraid to let herself trust him again.

Fearful she'd never get over Jared—and that'd make her life so bleak.

Billy arrived and he and Jared began preparing the front of the house for painting. Repairs were finished to the porch, so they removed the shutters and loose trim. Chipping away at peeling paint, patching gouge marks, masking the windows.

And that set the routine for the next week. Jared and Billy worked outside while Kelsey finished cleaning the downstairs rooms in preparation for painting and papering. She scrubbed down old paste, sized walls, masked trim and lay drop cloths.

In the evenings, Kelsey worked on Grandma's accounts. She and her part-time manager in Dallas talked via Skype each day so Kelsey felt she maintained an active role even with both she and Ellie away from the bakery.

Jared worked on the ranch books or spent hours with Jim learning as much as he could to make decisions concerning the ranch. He went to a Cattleman's Association meeting and Jim introduced him to other ranchers in the area.

Kelsey and Jared reached an uneasy truce regarding the office. A table was set up for Jared's use. Kelsey was very aware of Jared's every move when he was there, but he concentrated on his work and seemed to ignore her.

She wished she had that ability.

Ellie baked during the day and crocheted in the evenings, often spending the hours after dinner on the porch, enjoying the balmy nights or sitting in the kitchen with Kelsey while she baked.

Kelsey enjoyed their time together—and was relieved to avoid Jared.

She dwelt on the confrontation beneath the trees.

Had she misread the situation in London? He was so adamant nothing happened. She remembered what she'd seen, what the woman said.

And if she had it wrong, why hadn't he set her straight long ago?

Sam Clark came with his construction plans. Jared, Ellie and Kelsey all agreed on the plans as drafted and Sam received the go-ahead to begin construction. Kelsey expected Jared to make comments about where she'd come up with the money, but he never raised the issue.

The ground was leveled and the foundation poured.

Jared made daily trips to speak with the foreman and from time to time spend the day out with Jim or other cowboys. Riding out to study the land and the herd, he was taking an active role in running the ranch. And learning all he could.

"We're ready to start painting the house," Jared announced at lunch a week later. "Tomorrow morning. They've finally finished stirring up the dirt at the construction site, so we should be good to go. The weather forecast is for dry days ahead, so this is a window of opportunity we don't want to miss."

Kelsey looked up, smiling. "Great! It'll make such a difference. When that's finished, we can paint and paper the inside. The rooms are prepped and ready."

He nodded. "I've got three more cowboys committed to painting, so we'll be finished in a couple of days at the most. Then you and I can start on the downstairs rooms."

"What about your trip to Los Angeles? When are you two leaving?" Ellie asked.

"On Thursday. That gives us four days to do as much as we can."

Kelsey had almost forgotten about the proposed trip to Los Angeles. Dare she back out at this point? She opened her mouth to tell Jared she'd changed her mind, but he forestalled her.

"We'll leave early Thursday. We'll take your car, Kelsey, so you can take a suitcase. My bike isn't exactly conducive to luggage. We fly from Dallas mid day."

"She'll have to stop off at her apartment to get some clothes, too," Ellie said, eyeing her niece. "I'm sure she didn't bring anything suitable here."

Kelsey shut her mouth and dropped her gaze.

She'd discuss the situation with Ellie later. Get her to understand why she couldn't go—then tell Jared.

But later never arrived. Early the next morning Billy, Jim and two other cowboys arrived to erect long ladders around the house enabling them to reach the highest point.

Jared was surprised when Kelsey came out, her hair tied back, old clothes on. "I'm here to help," she said after meeting the cowboys.

"Okay, but not on the ladders. One of the men or I will do ladder work," Jared ordered Kelsey as the men began picking up paint buckets and rollers.

"I'll be fine," she said, not liking being bossed. It wasn't up to him to tell her what to do.

"You'll be fine as long as you do what I say," he replied mildly, studying the structure.

"And if I don't?"

She turned to challenge him head-on, hands on her hips. Her chin tilted.

"And if you don't I'll stop the process immediately. It's dangerous—stay away from the ladders."

He looked at her seriously.

"If it's so dangerous, why would you or Billy or one of the others go on them? You'd better not get hurt—you depend on your good looks for your career. If you got hurt, then what?"

He hesitated a moment and then nodded.

"If you must go to prove something, be careful. You can't bake cookies if you have a broken arm or leg."

Billy called and Jared turned away.

Painting the old house turned out to be fun. With Jim and Pete and Karl working and joking, the tension Kelsey felt around Jared vanished.

Throughout the day Jim told them stories of their uncle Henry and how he ran Windhaven Ranch. Jared shared stories of mishaps in his career and Kelsey recounted problems she encountered in starting up Grandma's.

Kelsey especially liked listening to Jared's vignettes. His acting ability gave each story its own special emphasis.

She felt as if she was there with him when he described them. She almost saw the other people, heard their voices when he altered his to imitate them.

She remembered the early television shows he'd been in, how well he'd done his parts. She hadn't seen any of his work in four years. He must be excellent to be in demand.

The trip to LA loomed ever closer.

And she still hadn't told him she wasn't going. She wouldn't be with him at the opening, wouldn't see if the audience liked the film, if he had another winner. She wouldn't be a part of the wild Hollywood crowd associated with movies done by his producer.

If she went, would she learn more about him?

Or be ignored while his fans and co-stars demanded his attention?

Seven

Jared drove Kelsey's car to Dallas. She directed him to the apartment she shared with Aunt Ellie in an old converted house that provided their ground floor flat with a spacious garden at the back.

Kelsey tried once more to persuade Jared that she shouldn't go, but he was having none of that. He wanted her to go—she said she would and he was holding her to that. End of discussion. He could be stubborn and implacable.

And Ellen stood with him and urging Kelsey to go.

"I have nothing to wear," she said as a last-ditch effort.

"I've got money. I'll buy you something," he'd replied easily.

"I don't want to go," she ground out between clenched teeth.

"Kelsey, I wanted to sell Windhaven. You want to keep it. I'm doing something that's not my choice. You can be gracious enough to do this for me."

His logic was irrefutable.

"Wait here," she said when he drew up in front of her apartment building.

She didn't want him seeing her place. She'd forever see him around Windhaven Ranch, on the porch, lounging by the kitchen table, riding his big Harley down the dusty road. She wanted to keep something free from memories of Jared. Not that it was likely she'd be living here much longer. Windhaven would be her home in the future.

As she hurried inside, she reviewed her wardrobe. She had nothing suitable for a gala opening night, nor the party she knew followed. The women who attended these affairs spent small fortunes on their gowns.

She pulled out a serviceable black dress, two suits to wear for her business meetings, and a casual dress for any other event. Packing in record time, she let herself out of the flat, still convinced this was a mistake.

The plane ride was short and they were met in Los Angeles by a chauffeur holding a card with Jared's name on it.

"From the studio—they send it for everyone," Jared explained as he introduced himself to the chauffeur.

It was nice to have someone else take care of luggage and transportation, Kelly thought as she scooted across the soft leather seat to make room for Jared in the stretch limo awaiting them.

She leaned back against the luxurious cushions and smiled. This was luxury and it was great. She glanced around in delight. The interior was the size of a small room. Opposite her seat was a tiny bar, a built-in TV and another bench seat. Soft music came from hidden speakers. The windows were tinted and private and the panel to the driver's area closed.

Jared joined her on the back seat and the door closed behind him.

Suddenly Kelsey didn't find the car spacious with Jared's presence. He moved towards the middle of the seat and leaned back, closing his eyes. His leg was close to hers, and she felt the cushions sag beneath his weight shifting her slightly toward him. Moving to the left cautiously, she tried to put more distance between them.

Jared opened his eyes lazily and looked at her. "Being close didn't used to bother you," he murmured audaciously.

Kelsey gave up the pretense and moved up against the far door.

"There's plenty of room in this car. We don't need to be in each other's laps."

"I can't think of a better place for you than in my lap. Come here, Kelsey." He patted the top of his thighs and smiled as if he knew what her response would be.

For an instant she considered doing it, if only to shock him out of his complacent, patronizing attitude. Show him that he didn't know her as well as he thought he did.

But she didn't.

"No thanks."

She turned and gazed out of the window as the airport fell behind and they took the crowded afternoon freeway into Los Angeles. The tall glass and steel buildings in the distance gleamed in the afternoon sun. The air was smoggy, nothing new for LA.

She missed the cleaner air of Windhaven.

She jumped when Jared's fingers traced down her

arm. Swiveling round to him, she looked puzzled.

"I'm wondering what you're smiling about. The thought of sitting in my lap?" he asked lazily, his hand capturing hers, threading his fingers through hers.

She frowned. "I wasn't smiling."

His touch disturbed her. Once again the familiar pull of attraction flared, his fingers awakening nerve-endings, her body longing for more than a casual clasping of hands. Not that her hand in his felt casual. His fingers were warm, strong, wrapped snugly around hers, his thumb brushing gently back and forth across the back of her hand.

"You were," he said as she tugged her hand to free herself.

Jared tugged in return, and tipped her towards him. In only a moment, he scooped her up and deposited her in his lap, his hands on her hips, holding her in place.

"Let me go!" she said frowning at him.

"Relax, I'm only going to kiss you. I've kissed you before."

"I don't want—"

His mouth stopped her. His kiss stopped her heart. But only for a second, then it surged back beating faster than ever.

She sighed softly and gave in, kissing him back.

His lips were hot, claiming her mouth, exploring the softness.

She encircled his neck with her arms, her fingers moving through the thick dark hair that grew a little long. The movement brought her snug against the strength of his chest. Beneath her hip she felt Jared. He wanted her and the knowledge excited her further.

Moving on the wide seat, Jared shifted their positions slightly so that Kelsey was almost lying on top of him. Her mouth clung to his, her hands now tracing the muscles of his shoulders, the firm column of his neck, slipping beneath the collar of his shirt to the heat of his body.

His hand slipped beneath her top, sweeping over her back, his fingers like icy fire as he followed her spine, feathering caresses against her fevered skin. She moved against him, trying to get closer, her mouth on fire, her body on fire.

The car swerved and drew to a halt.

"Blast it all!"

Jared sat her beside him on the seat, running his hands through his hair as he looked out of the window at the entrance to the Regent Hotel. He quickly glanced at her.

"We're here faster than I thought we'd be."

Kelsey was unable to look at him, unable to accept the fact she'd participated with him in lovemaking in the back of a moving car. The privacy glass was between them and the driver, but could he have seen anything?

Her cheeks burned with embarrassment.

Jared noted her flustered appearance.

"Relax. The windows are tinted, so no one saw anything."

The warmth she'd felt only moments before fled, to be replaced with dread. Surely he didn't see this as changing anything?

The door opened and Jared stepped out, turning to offer Kelsey a hand. She ignored it, climbing out on her own and letting her eyes scan the front of the imposing building.

The hotel was near the city center. She followed the hotel bellman into the lobby, her eyes widening at the interior.

A three-story atrium rose over the gleaming marble lobby floor. Green ivy and ferns spilled from each floor's balustrade, cascading down for several feet, giving the atrium an open-air aspect. The coolness was fresh and welcomed after the smoggy LA air.

Kelsey's gaze took in the ornate marble benches, the comfortable chairs and sofas clustered around small tables. Tall potted trees scattered in the lobby continued the open-air theme of the atrium. The atmosphere was subdued, elegant and sophisticated.

Jared turned from the registration desk and handed her a key.

"Yours."

Without waiting to see if she followed, he turned and headed for the elevators.

Not wanting to be left behind, Kelsey hurried after him. The bellmen held the elevator door for them both, then entered with his cart carrying only Kelsey's bag.

"Jared, where's your luggage?" she asked as the elevator silently rose.

"Someone from the studio brought it. The celebratory party's here tonight and for safety's sake, the studio's putting us all up here. No possibility of accidents after the event."

The doors opened soundlessly and the bellmen smiled as he motioned them to step out.

Jared took Kelsey's hand and led her down the hall, pausing before room 3412. Taking her key, he opened the door and ushered her inside, the bellman right behind.

The sitting room was bright with light flooding in from the floor-to-ceiling windows. The panorama view of LA was blurred somewhat by the thick smog. On a clear day the San Gabriel mountains could be seen. Not today.

"This is beautiful," she murmured in delight at the elegance of the room, glad to have something to say. Then she had a sudden thought.

"A suite?"

"The studio's picking up the tab. Glad you like it."

Jared closed the door behind the bellman and turned to face Kelsey.

"What's going on?" she asked trying to come up with an idea that would be acceptable.

Not jumping to the obvious conclusion that presented itself.

"Two bedrooms," he said, not moving from the door. "One for you—" he pointed to the left "—and one for me." He pointed to the door on the right. "If you want to get your own room, go for it. The suite's provided by the studio, no charge.

With that he gave a careless shrug and moved to open the door to his bedroom. He closed it behind him without another word.

Kelsey stared after him, indecision confusing her.

Did he mean it? Or was it some sort of scheme to lure her into a comfort level that—that what?

He wouldn't do anything she didn't allow.

She took her suitcase and went to her room.

Now what? she thought as she hung up her few dresses and suits in the spacious wardrobe. The opening was tomorrow night. Until then, was she on her own.

She'd called Peter Marcus from the ranch and set an appointment for the following morning. Aunt Ellie was right. This was a perfect way to take advantage of this opportunity.

Nothing to do today regarding business. She had the rest of the day free. What to do?

His sharp knock on her door startled her. Warily she walked over and opened it.

He pushed past her as if he had every right and threw open the doors to her wardrobe.

"What do you want?" she asked, her hand gripping the doorknob.

"Checking out your clothes for tomorrow night. Is this the best you came up with?"

He dragged the black dress from the hanger and held it before him, shaking it before he studied it from shoulder to hem.

"Yes. It's perfectly acceptable."

Acceptable wouldn't compete with the glamour of the others at the opening, but it was the best she had for such a gala event. She rarely mingled in such exalted circles. The few dresses that would be more appropriate were at her mother's house. There'd been no time to send for one of them.

"Come on, we're going shopping."

"Jared, I'm not—"

"Oh, yes, you are." He loomed over her, his eyes narrowed. "This event is important to me and I want you to look as if you belong. You'll feel better, too. This thing—" he waved the dress before her "—will only make you look like a crow in the midst of colorful birds of paradise. You'd be miserable and that's not going to happen. Let's go."

"I'm perfectly capable of buying myself a dress," she said.

Maybe she should reconsider the evening. It was obvious he wanted her to uphold some glamorous image suitable for a movie star's date.

"I want to buy you a pretty dress. Can't a husband buy his wife a dress?"

She hesitated a moment longer, not sure the entreaty in his voice was genuine.

"Kelsey?"

She looked up at the gentle entreaty in his voice. A muscle jerked in his cheek. Despite his irritation, he kept his voice gentle.

"All right." She nodded, giving in.

The dress was gorgeous. She liked it the moment he picked it off the rack and held it up to her. They'd taken a short cab ride to Rodeo Drive and then walked along the street, gazing into windows. This elegant boutique had displayed fewer dresses than others, but each was unique and special.

He held it before her, tilting his head as if envisaging her wearing it. It was deep, iridescent blue, shimmering in the light as the soft material moved in the air.

"Try it on," he said, handing it to her.

Kelsey loved it when she saw herself in the mirror. The deep V neckline plunged in front, the shadow of her cleavage clearly visible in the dressing-room mirror, her arms bare. The material clung to her figure like a lover and felt like silk when she moved. The skirt flared and ended above her knees, displaying her legs to full advantage. This particular shade of blue deepened the color in her eyes. It was perfect.

And probably cost the earth.

"Are you going to let me see?" Jared materialized beside her in the mirror, holding a pink dress. He hung it on a hook.

Kelsey turned slowly, feeling beautiful, smiling as she faced him and let him look at her.

Her throat tightened at his look. His gaze roved over her, lingering on the swell of her breasts, the tanned legs displayed so well beneath the hem.

When he met her eyes, his were blank, giving no indication of his thoughts.

"Take it."

He left the dressing room.

The pink gown was also beautiful, not as short and more demure. She liked it, too, and wondered if he wanted her to choose.

When she was dressed in her own clothes, the saleswoman took both dresses from the dressing-room and smiled at Kelsey. In only moments she knew why. Jared bought both.

"I can't let you—"

"Kelsey."

He placed a finger across her lips, lingering a moment longer than was necessary as if he enjoyed touching her.

"Shut up. I don't want to hear any more what you

can't do or won't do. Take the blasted dresses and give me some peace. And find a fancy pair of shoes to go with them. I'd like to head back to the hotel soon."

Two beautiful dresses—it was wonderful.

When they entered the lobby of the Regent Hotel a half hour later, Jared was hailed by a young man who stood up quickly from a sofa where he'd been sitting, watching for them. He hurried over.

"Jared, hi. When did you get here?"

The man was tall and lanky, with long brown hair tied back in a ponytail. Jeans and boots seemed at odds with his pale blue dress shirt and tie.

"Jerry, good to see you."

Jared reached out the shake hands.

"We got in earlier today. This is my cousin, Kelsey Adams. Kelsey, this is Jerry Longstreet, stunt director of my last two films."

Kelsey shook hands, stunned by the introduction. She flicked a quick look at Jared, but he continued chatting with Jerry. After all his grand talk about reclaiming his wife, he didn't introduce her as such.

Why not?

She thought the entire reason for her attending the opening was to let the world know he was married.

"Jared!"

Kelsey swung around at the familiar feminine voice. It was the woman from the phone call.

A beautiful woman with hair the color of spun gold smiled as she and an older man approached, her eyes only on Jared.

"Pamela."

Jared kissed her cheek when she came up to him and gave her a brief hug.

"Peter, good to see you."

He shook hands with the studio executive accompanying her.

Kelsey felt a jolt of jealousy pierce at the sight of Jared kissing Pamela. Was this the reason Jared referred to her as his cousin?

The woman was beautiful.

Jared introduced Kelsey to Pamela, his leading lady in the last film and the one about to begin.

The four of them drifted towards the bar, Kelsey with them.

Jared turned to her and handed her the packages he'd carried from their shopping.

"We'll be talking about the new film. It'll be boring for you. Why don't you get your hair done or something and I'll pick you up for dinner around seven."

As a dismissal, it was the most abrupt one she'd had in a long time.

No one else seemed to see anything amiss, however, and she forced a smile on her face.

"Fine."

It was obvious he didn't want her there she couldn't believe he hadn't said it aloud.

She shouldn't have come to LA. She'd known that from the first time he'd mentioned it.

"Seven o'clock and wear the pink dress."

He turned and walked away.

Kelsey was a nervous wreck by the time seven o'clock rolled around. She'd had her hair done, only because it was time for a trim, not because Jared suggested it. She was pleased with the style. She'd even had her make-up done.

And now all that trouble for what? To eat room service in the room by herself? If he didn't show up soon, that would be the default for dinner.

"Kelsey, I'm running a little late. I'll be ready in twenty minutes," Jared's voice called from the sitting room when he entered the suite.

So dinner was still on. She took a deep breath and left the safety of her room. Opening the door to the sitting room, she stepped in and spoke a trifle loudly.

"I don't think I want to go," she said.

He paused halfway into his room and spun around.

"Now what?" His eyes took in the new hairstyle, the make-up and the shorts she wore.

"I agreed to attend the opening with you, not be at your beck and call the entire trip."

She'd rehearsed the line all afternoon.

"Peter, Pamela and Jerry are going to dinner with us. I thought you'd like a nice evening out. If you don't wish to go, fine by me."

"You won't miss me."

"They wanted a chance to get to know you."

"As your cousin?" she said, not knowing the words would be blurted out like that.

She didn't like the smile on Jared's face.

"Did that rankle, sweetheart?" he said softly, watching her.

"Confused me is more likely." She raised her chin, refusing to let him see it had bothered her. "At

135

Windhaven you introduced me to Jim as your wife, here as your cousin. Which is it going to be?"

"You are my cousin, however distant. Besides, it saves explanations. Most people in Hollywood don't know I'm married."

"That's because you don't act it," she snapped out.

He walked over to her, holding her gaze every step. Leaning over until his eyes were on a level with hers, he spoke slowly.

"I do not go to any parties that are not required for business and do not date other women!"

She was unprepared for the flash of pain she saw in his eyes. He turned so abruptly that Kelsey wondered if she'd imagined it.

"Come tonight or don't come, I don't care any more," he said rubbing his eyes with one hand.

The door closed behind him. Kelsey was left alone in the middle of the room, doubts and questions flooding.

Several long minutes later she turned around and went to her room to put on the pink dress. She questioned her sanity, but decided she did want to learn more about his life. Meet his business colleagues.

She waited by the window in the sitting room, watching the changing colors of the sky as night approached. When the knock came, she glanced at Jared's closed door and went to open the suite door.

"Kelsey, isn't it? We didn't have time to talk this afternoon. Men are so bossy, aren't they? You look nice. Are we late?"

Pamela drifted in with a sweet smile. Jerry Longstreet was behind her, looking quite the professional businessman in his suit and wingtip shoes, despite the tied-back hair.

"Actually Jared's running late. Would you care for some wine?"

She'd noticed two bottles in the small bar that afternoon.

"Not for me. How about you, darling?" Pamela called over her shoulder as she went to the window and gazed out over the view.

"No, I'm good," Jerry responded.

Jared came from his bedroom, dressed in a dark suit, white shirt and red tie. He greeted Pamela and Jerry.

"Isn't Peter joining us?"

"He'll meet us there," Jerry said.

Kelsey stared at Jared, unable to help herself.

He looked fabulous. His dark suit and crisp white shirt gave him a formality missing on the ranch. His hair was tamed and his demeanor cosmopolitan. He looked like a successful, powerful businessman. She usually saw him dressed in more casual attire, which made him more approachable. Now she felt almost intimidated.

As they waited for the elevator a few minutes later, Pamela tucked her hand in Jared's arm and smiled over at Kelsey.

"So tell me, darling, how did you get Jared to include you in this supper tonight? You're the first girl he's brought since I've known him. We were wondering about his being such a loner."

Jared chuckled at that and watched Kelsey's startled expression.

"Don't you know? She's the girl from back home. He

likes Texas girls, not you brash Californians," Jerry said, pulling her hand from Jared's arm and tucking it in his.

Pamela smiled at him and at Jared. Kelsey wanted to step between them, but kept her place, dismayed at the jealousy that flared.

Jared had been the reason for the end of their relationship four years ago. She had no hold on him.

Did he truly not date?

Or was he super discreet?

When Jared's friends discovered she operated Grandma Mary's Cookies, they told her they recognized the name from the boxes of cookies Jared often had on the set.

Kelsey didn't expect that.

"Mom sends them. She didn't mention they were yours," he said. "Afraid I wouldn't eat them if she told me they were from you, I guess."

"They're great cookies," Jerry said, his smile gentle.

Kelsey smiled in return.

"You can try them right out of the oven when you come to the ranch," Jared said.

"They're coming to the ranch?" Kelsey asked, a sinking suspicion growing.

"There's been a setback on the filming schedule. The location for most of the outside shots is burning as we speak. California has major forest fires every year. Nothing can escape the conflagration once it starts. And it takes days and weeks to put it out."

Kelsey nodded. Everyone knew about the California wild fires. But she hadn't realized one was burning the location for the movie.

"It's ruined the location for the film. I've invited some of the planning crew up to see the ranch. If the location will work, we'll use it. Nothing's decided yet. We need to see if the landscape will be suitable. If so, then there'd be a ton of work to get logistics planned, alter the shooting schedule, rearrange all the travel itineraries. But at least it's one option to consider," Jared explained.

"I see." Kelsey tried to ignore the spurt of jealousy as she looked at Pamela. "Are you coming also to visit us?"

"Us?" Pamela looked surprised.

"Kelsey and I inherited Windhaven Ranch jointly. She's moving the baking production for Grandma Mary's Cookies there. She bakes other things as well—cinnamon rolls that melt in your mouth for one. I bet we can get her to make some for breakfast. They're fantastic."

"Well, what a nice surprise. We might stay forever, right, darling?" Pamela smiled at Jared, then at Jerry. "I love sweets."

Eight

Kelsey didn't see Jared the next morning before her meeting with Markham Enterprises. She slipped out of their suite before he woke. She took a cab the short distance to the glass and steel high-rise building that housed Markham Enterprises.

Joseph Markham was the driving force behind the boutique specialty business that had branches in most of the major hotels in the southwest. He'd tasted the cookies on a trip to Dallas and liked them enough to want to include in his shops.

"Tourists especially love that kind of thing," he said as they completed the deal. "People splurge when on vacation. Or if they can add things to business expense accounts. Your cookies always taste so fresh, not like they're weeks old by the time someone buys them."

Kelsey was careful about quality control—and she didn't want to lose that distinction, no matter how appealing expansion appeared.

She and Joseph Markham discussed terms and delivery dates. She was excited to expand her business into such a high-end market—as long as she had the new kitchen which could produce the amount she was committing to.

Pleased with the consummation of the deal, they shared a fine luncheon in the restaurant on the top floor of the building where Markham Enterprises was headquartered. It was after two when Kelsey finished, and she was reluctant to return to the hotel.

Taking a cab to Palisades Park, she found a quiet bench and sat down to enjoy the peaceful afternoon as she had planned to do yesterday. The sun was warm, the breeze from the ocean refreshing without being cold. The view from the park of the Pacific and the cliffs where land met the ocean were spectacular. She relaxed and enjoyed the peace and beauty.

Time enough later to worry about Jared and his presence at the ranch. Which would be worse if the movie was filmed on site. He could end up staying for a year.

When the afternoon breeze picked up, she returned to the hotel. The suite was quiet when she entered. On her door she found a note taped. "Be ready at 8, Jared".

She pushed open the door to her room and paused. On her bed was a dark fake-fur wrap, perfect for the cool evening air. How thoughtful of him to provide that for her as well as the dress. Why? Was it to give her something pretty—or was he trying to bribe his way back into her good graces?

She closed her door and drew her curtains. Trailing her fingers across the jacket, feeling its softness, she smiled in delight. Who cared? For tonight she'd wear it and be happy.

Taking off her dress, she pulled back the comforter

on her bed. Lying down, she relaxed, feeling tense muscles give way to the soothing support of the bed. The night would be long, and she'd already had a busy day. A short nap would set her up for the evening.

As her eyes closed, recent scenes with Jared drifted past her lids. His arrival at Windhaven on the powerful motorcycle. His broad shoulders stretching the cotton fabric of his T-shirt. The angry forfeit he'd claimed in the kitchen. And the long, delightful, heady moments in the limousine from the airport. Remembering that scene most of all, Kelsey fell asleep.

"Are you ill?" Jared's voice awoke her, sounding concerned.

Kelsey frowned, reluctant to wake up, wanting to snuggle back down in the bed and continue with the dreams she was enjoying. But he wouldn't let her.

"Kelsey."

He shook her shoulder gently.

Opening her eyes, Kelsey stared into Jared's worried gaze.

"Are you ill?" he asked again, placing the back of his hand against her forehead, against her cheek.

She shook her head.

"I wanted to stay awake however late we were tonight, so I took a nap. What time is it?"

She tried to see the clock on the table. With the curtains drawn the room was dim, almost dark. She couldn't make out the numerals.

Jared sat down, his hip pressing against hers through the comforter as he sat on the edge of the bed. The mattress dipped towards him and Kelsey couldn't move away. Her eyes never left his face though she schooled her features to give nothing away, nothing of the turmoil and excitement coursing through her at his proximity.

"It's not even seven. Plenty of time to get ready. I knocked when I got in. When I got no response, I peeked in. You worried me. I didn't expect to find you in bed."

"I'm fine. Just tired."

Wide awake now, though, with nerves stretched to breaking-point. She shifted her gaze lest he read her mind.

The lacy edge of her slip caressed the mounds of her breasts and drew Jared's gaze. Kelsey felt the tension rise in him and longed to snatch the comforter to her throat, but pride held her back. She didn't need to let him know how much his presence disturbed her.

There was no reason for it. She made her position clear. She was no longer interested in Jared Martin. The next time he kissed her she'd remain passive, aloof. That'd prove to him that she was impervious to his charm.

Liar, a little voice inside her asserted.

"How did the deal with Markham Enterprises go?" he asked, loath to leave the quiet intimacy of her room.

She glanced at him, surprised. Did he care?

"Fine."

She refused to be drawn into exchanging confidences. She wished the renovations at Windhaven were complete and she'd convince him to sell her his share.

The thought filled her with sadness.

"What's the matter, love?" Jared asked brushing his fingertips beneath her eyes, seeing the sadness in her eyes.

"Nothing. Go and get dressed. I'll be ready by eight," she said, almost holding her breath, afraid he'd kiss her.

And if he did, could she pretend she didn't care? It was too dangerous, she in bed, he beside her.

His gaze dropped to the edge of her slip and his hand came up. One finger lightly skimmed across the top of the lace. She held her breath, tingling at his touch.

"Don't you ever wear a bra?" His murmur was so low she almost missed it. Was he talking to her or himself?

She tried to see his expression, but the room was dim. He was looking at the white slip against her skin, then felt his fingers brushing against her warm skin.

"Oh, Kelsey, love, it's been so long."

He leaned over and kissed her. Heat curled deep within her and she couldn't move away from him at that moment if the world threatened to end.

Her hands threaded themselves in his thick dark hair, knowing she should be pushing him away, but rejoicing in the feel of him.

She needed to stop. But she lost that thought and all others while floating on the erotic sensations Jared created with his lips.

He broke off his kiss to pull back a few inches, gazing down at her with passionate eyes. She stared back at him, knowing he'd see what delight he ignited within her. Deep within her a burning need was building. He saw it in her eyes.

She'd forgotten the mindless, earth-shattering pleasure and enchantment his touch brought. He set the pace and she followed. His hands touched her everywhere, hot and cold, strong and gentle. She responded to his touch as the flowers responded to the sun.

When Jared brought her to the height of ecstasy she repeated his name over and over and clung to him reveling in the glory he brought them both, feeling the heat at such a fiery level it threatened to consume them.

Jared was more than content to hold her, touch her, cradle her against him. As he had longed to do for so many long empty years.

But duty called. He had to go to the opening. It was his primary reason for being in Los Angeles. He had to be there tonight.

"Kelsey?" His voice was as soft as dark velvet.

"Mmm?"

She kept her eyes closed. The enchantment hadn't worn off.

"We don't have much time to get dressed. We need to leave by eight."

Even as he spoke, he made no effort to move.

"I don't want to go," she said, burrowing against him.

"I have to, Kelsey. Come with me."

He pulled back a few inches to kiss her again.

"I did get a new dress," she said softly, her eyes still closed.

"Yes."

He kissed her and moved to pull away. Her arms tightened, then with a sigh she let them slide from him. When he moved away, the cool air hit her skin where he'd been so hot. She turned over and curled up, trying to recapture the warmth.

"Get up, Kelsey. Get dressed."

He kissed her cheek and she heard him leave.

She refused to think. Slowly she climbed out of bed

and went for a short shower. She'd think about it later. They had to go to the preview and the party afterwards.

Dressed in the iridescent blue dress with its dramatic and daring neckline, hair tamed after her romp in bed, make-up artfully touched up, Kelsey was ready to face the event.

And questioned her sanity constantly, despite her earnest efforts to delay thinking.

Why was she doing this? To get another glimpse of Jared's life, to make a memory to cherish after he'd gone? To understand him better?

Or for the sake of spending more time with him, knowing their time together now was running out?

Had this afternoon changed things somehow? Or was it only another incident for him? Was he dallying with her as he had with that other woman in London?

Kelsey's eyes became stricken as she stared back at herself in the mirror.

No, she refused to think about anything until later. Tonight she was determined to enjoy herself. Live in the present, not the future, she admonished herself as she picked up the fake-fur jacket and tried it on over her dress.

It was perfect, soft and warm. And it'd be perfect to ward off the cool LA nights. How thoughtful of him to think of it, to know she'd need something like this.

She should have thanked him.

She felt shy when she joined him in the main room of the suite. They were pushing the deadline and Jared was in no mood to linger. He rushed her down to the limo and directed the driver to the theater. It was a short distance away, no time for any talk.

Kelsey felt a sense of deja vu when the limousine pulled up before the ornate El Capitan Theater. She'd seen news clips from other movie premieres where crowds thronged the sidewalks while the stars arrived one after another. This was no different.

She felt the sheer excitement of everyone there. Fans called out compliments to Jared. It was a gala opening.

She allowed the driver to assist her from the limo and waited for Jared to join her, wondering again how she'd let herself be talked into this.

People clapped and called out to Jared. The news media snapped picture after picture, always with flashes to brighten the evening light.

Kelsey shrank back, wishing once again that she hadn't come. She didn't like crowds or large parties where she knew no one.

Jared smiled and waved to the people lining the red carpet and led Kelsey into the large lobby with the pink marble floor and vaulted gilt ceilings. The celebrities and society of Los Angeles, invited for the viewing and to the party afterwards, were present, mingling, talking, laughing and enjoying themselves. It was a madhouse! Kelsey marveled that so many people fit in one finite place and could still move around.

"See anyone you know?" Jared said in her ear, his arm firmly round her waist as she gazed around the large lobby—anchoring her to his side so that she wouldn't get lost.

Kelsey shook her head. She saw a throng of people. All the women were dressed to the nines, diamonds and rubies and emeralds sparkling in the chandelier light. The gowns were long and short, sedate and flamboyant, all the beautiful colors of the rainbow. Most of the men were in dinner-jackets like Jared, looking distinguished and impressive.

"Do you?"

She moved closer to him. Glad he'd bought the gown she wore. She didn't feel out of.

"Not yet. But the whole crew's here. We'll find them soon."

"Who's doing this?" she asked, watching the people talk and laugh and greet each other. Champagne flowed freely.

"The crowd? Tri-Color Pictures wants to make a big push with this film. We're hoping it'll do well here, open to rave reviews so everyone will flock to see it."

Kelsey looked up at him with guilt written on her face.

"Jared, I don't even know the title or what it's about."

He laughed and shook his head, smiling down at her.

"At least you're not after me for the glory. Wait and see, then. Come on, I see Kyle Robertson, one of the other actors."

She reminded him she wasn't after him at all, but Jared ignored her comment, laced his fingers through hers and led the way through the crowd towards someone in the distance.

In only a few minutes Kelsey and Jared were in the midst of a cheerful group from Tri-Color Pictures. They were friendly, happy and excited for the release of their project.

Kelsey relaxed and began to feel comfortable among them. Gone was the painful shyness she'd experienced the few times she'd gone to parties with Jared when they'd first been married. Tonight was totally different. She listened, laughed and enjoyed herself, conscious all the while of Jared's fingers entwined with hers.

The two of them were subject to speculative glances from the others, but everyone was too polite to say anything.

Once Kelsey almost laughed aloud at the thought of the questions and speculation that had to be sweeping through the group. Then she sobered. It was not funny. What was she going to do? Remembering their afternoon brought warmth and color to her cheeks, and her heart pounded again.

The movie was a surprise, a swashbuckler of the finest order. Jared starred as an English convict wrongly sent to Australia for beating the villain. He quickly fought his way out of servitude and into the shipping trade. Becoming a wealthy man, he returned to England to capture the heart of the woman he loved, and expose the villain for the criminal he was, thus vindicating his own conviction.

It was fast-paced, action-packed and exciting. The love interest caused a surge of jealousy to pulse through Kelsey as she watched Jared kiss Pamela as if she was the most precious thing in the world.

He'd kissed her that way only a few hours ago. Had that been an act?

Or might she have been wrong? Was Ellie right? Might there be another explanation for the scene she'd walked in on that fateful morning?

She glanced at Jared from beneath her lashes. Dared

she ask him again? Did she really want to know? How could he explain away what she'd seen?

The pain pricked her afresh, especially sharp after this afternoon.

Pushing the thoughts away, she tried to enjoy the movie and let the past go. At least for tonight.

Peter Marshall, the picture's producer, met them after the film as they entered the huge ballroom at the hotel where the party had already started. He greeted everyone as they came in, giving Jared a warm handshake.

"The opening went well, Jared. Early reports are the critics love it."

He beamed as his gaze darted around the huge ballroom, ascertaining that everything was continuing to proceed according to plan.

Kelsey was amused to note he looked exactly like her idea of a successful movie mogul—sleek, sophisticated and proudly puffing out his chest.

But he had every right to be proud: the film was excellent—entertaining, romantic, breathtaking and action-filled. She knew they had a winner on their hands.

"Come on, Jared, I see some backers and potential backers I want you to meet."

Peter nodded to several gentlemen across the floor.

As Jared waited for Kelsey to precede him, Peter shook his head.

"No, no. Your cousin'll be bored. We'll be back soon, little lady. Help yourself to some champagne. Enjoy the party."

He winked at Kelsey and took Jared by the arm.

For a moment she thought he wouldn't budge, but,

with a shrug and a quick look at Kelsey, Jared walked away with Peter.

Feeling alone and adrift, Kelsey made her way to one of the heavily laden tables. The hors d'oeuvres were plentiful and Kelsey sampled different ones which were familiar—crab puffs, caviar, cheese swirls.

"Jared gone missing?"

Jerry Longstreet came up to her, an empty plate in his hand, a rueful smile on his face. He loaded a fresh supply of canapes on his plate.

"He went to meet with some backers."

"Pamela, too. They don't need stunt directors to meet backers. Which is just as well—I don't like business."

"I do. I have my own."

"I know. Cookies. Maybe that wouldn't be a bad business. Come over to the sidelines and let's talk. And not about movies and box-office receipts or scripts. I think maybe I'll switch to still photography and film Yosemite like Ansel Adams did."

Kelsey smiled uncertainly, wondering if he was serious or teasing, but she followed him to the edge of the dance-floor. Small tables were scattered around and they found an empty one.

"Really? Yosemite?" she asked when seated.

"No. I'm mouthing off. End-of-film blues. I'd rather be home safe and sound with my wife and our kids. I hate traveling if it's not for work."

"I thought this was for work, promoting the film."

"It is, but I'd still rather be home."

He finished the last of the small tidbits and sat back in his chair, a mournful look on his face.

Kelsey grinned.

"Tell me about your children."

She empathized with his feelings. She felt out of place and eager to leave. It was suddenly too much like the other parties she'd gone to before. Once he left her on her own, all the sparkle vanished and it was just a group of strangers having a good time around her.

While Jerry regaled her with tales of his two little daughters, Kelsey scanned the ballroom, looking for Jared, listening to Jerry with only half an ear.

When at last she saw Jared, she wished she hadn't.

The crowd parted, and at the opposite side of the room Jared and Pamela stood in the midst of a group of men. Without warning, Jared leaned over and kissed Pamela, who enthusiastically threw her arms around him.

Kelsey stared. The pain pierced her heart like a knife. If she'd had a moment's hesitation about her relationship with Jared, if she'd ever considered trying again, it just ended.

"It means nothing, you know," Jerry said, observing her expression.

Kelsey turned back to look at him, the hurt still evident in her eyes.

"It's for show for the producers, for the backers, for the paparazzi. You're smitten with Jared, aren't you?"

Kelsey's eyes dropped to the tablecloth, and she stared at the snowy whiteness for a long moment before replying.

"Does it show?"

Was that why he'd made love to her today, because he knew she still loved him?

"Well, you have this look about you and it's not cousinly, more like the look my wife gives me sometimes, when she's not mad at me." He grinned and shrugged, "Does Jared know?" he asked.

"No, and don't you tell him."

She glared at him, helpless if he told. Heat rose in her cheeks. She didn't want Jared to know. She hadn't said anything that afternoon except his name.

And he'd said nothing either, she realized with a sinking feeling.

Jerry drew a forefinger across his lips, then made a locking motion. "My lips are sealed. He will never learn the deep, dark secret from me, oh fair one."

Kelsey smiled at his nonsense, knowing instantly that she trusted him. Anyone so crazy about his kids couldn't be a snitch.

"Dance?" Jerry asked as the music started up again.

"I'd love to."

Kelsey refused to let her eyes wander towards Jared. She didn't want to know if he and Pamela were kissing again. Or if they'd slipped away.

Her heart contracted with the thought. She'd been a fool this afternoon—made a mistake not soon repeated!

The melody was haunting, but the way Jerry danced wasn't. Kelsey was having fun. He was entertaining and amusing, telling her tall tales about the cast members, their foibles, superstitions.

"And do you share in those?"

"I'm an artist, we're allowed," Jerry said pompously.

Kelsey laughed.

"I hope I'm interrupting something."

Jared's cool voice broke into their conversation, his eyes dark, narrowed in anger at Jerry.

"Only a dance with a very nice lady. Go find your own partner," Jerry said, spinning Kelsey away from Jared.

To no avail—in only two seconds a firm hand gripped Jerry's shoulder. "You go find your partner. Kelsey's mine."

The music ended, stalling a confrontation.

"Well, then. Maybe I'll hunt up Pamela and see if she needs moral support from the kiss-'em-and-leave-'em hero."

Jared watched Jerry walk away, then swung back to Kelsey.

"And that meant?"

"Nothing." She was glad of the calmness that invaded her, the even timbre of her voice. "We saw you and Pamela in a clinch. He thought I'd take it wrong."

She didn't raise her eyes above his throat, afraid of what she'd see, afraid of what Jared would see in her.

"Blast it!" Jared said softly.

Before he said anything further, two other guests approached him to compliment him on the film, discuss other roles they had enjoyed him playing.

The rest of the night was more of the same. Jared's fans and associates came up to congratulate him on the fine performance, to discuss the box office appeal, and to theorize on future films.

He and Kelsey didn't have a moment alone.

Each time Kelsey tried to escape, Jared restrained her—an arm across her shoulders, drawing her hand into the crook of his arm, reaching down to grasp her hand, lacing his fingers through hers. Through it all he ignored the whispers those gestures caused.

Once again the party began to sparkle.

She enjoyed being with him, letting him capture the glory for his performance, content to be near, to see how well others thought of his talent.

She chatted easily with different people, from the studio cast to crew members and residents of California's largest city. Her feelings of shyness fled and Kelsey actually enjoyed herself.

Nine

As the reception wound down, Peter invited his two stars to a short night cap in one of the hotel's bars.

They were soon settled at a large table in one of the corners of the Shangri-la Bar.

"Well, darlings, it went very well, don't you think?" Pamela asked everyone, her smile beautiful, her enthusiasm contagious.

"Yes, yes, it did." Peter sat in his corner, a happy, contented smile never leaving his face.

Kelsey imagined she saw the dollar signs in his eyes.

"I think I love LA. Fans are so appreciative," Pamela said extravagantly.

"Not for everyone, sweet," Jerry said lazily, his eyes closed, head leaning back.

Pamela smiled at Jared. "I can't wait for tomorrow when we leave for Windhaven," she said seductively. "Will I like Texas as much as California?"

"Jared, I won't be able to make it after all, my boy, not really my style anyway. That talk with Barlow should show some positive results. The logistical staff will give me the information I need to determine if the ranch is a suitable alternative. I expect to see all of you back in LA by the end of the month. We have a lot to do for the next one. Can't rest on our laurels, you know," Peter said as their drinks arrived.

Kelsey remained silent, sipping her rum and coke. Nothing had changed. He was barreling ahead offering the ranch to the movie company without even asking her. She owned fifty percent. What if she drew a line in the house and wouldn't let any of his friends cross it? She almost laughed at the absurdity.

Finally the group broke up.

"You're quiet," Jared said as they shared the elevator to their floor.

"Talked out."

She was dead tired, and her feet ached—and her heart. All she wanted was to escape to the sanctity of her room and the oblivion of sleep. And think about what changes would happen if they ended up filming the next movie on the ranch.

He'd be gone by the end of the month. But that didn't look as if it was going to happen.

She'd come to terms with her life without him and wanted that contentment again.

"I thought you might be upset about something," Jared said, opening the door to the suite and motioning Kelsey to precede him.

"I can't believe you invited all those people to Windhaven without asking me about it. We're in the middle of renovations, so the house is a mess. The foundation for the new kitchen will be ready to build upon. Which makes it highly unlikely guests will enjoy the commotion. And when I expect to be flat out busy, we're expected to entertain guests?" she blurted out.

Anger and hurt flared whenever she thought of Pamela and Jared together. She wished she'd fought him this afternoon, not found such delight in his arms.

Or wished she stayed in her dream world a little longer, paid strict attention to Jerry and never seen Jared and Pamela at the party.

"Pamela said she's never been to Texas. She practically invited herself."

"And Jerry—did you invite him along for me?" she bit out, trying to move away.

A small smile touched the corners of Jared's mouth and he reached out to hold Kelsey's shoulders lightly, a gleam in his eye.

"Only if you think Pamela's for me."

His voice was silky, his eyes dancing in the lamplight.

"I don't care who's for you. I'm not."

"I know you saw the kiss."

She tried to move, but his hands tightened.

"It was only a friendly kiss because of the new deal for a film. We'll star together again. Are you jealous, Kel?"

"No." But her eyes didn't meet his.

"I've got plenty of kisses for you, Kelsey, if you want them."

His voice was low and seductive. For a moment she blinked, then thought of the movie. He was an actor, after all. This was probably a part to him. Play it well and what would he get? Was that what he'd done earlier?

The shaft of pain was almost too much to bear.

"I want to go to bed."

"Now we're making progress," he said audaciously.

She met his eyes at that, hers stricken, his dancing in amusement.

"I didn't mean together—with you," she said quickly.

"You didn't say that earlier today, sweet Kelsey." He leaned over and kissed her.

Kelsey wanted to protest, to pull away. She didn't want him to kiss her after Pamela. She wanted to return to Windhaven and finish all the work so that Jared would leave.

But when his mouth touched hers she was lost. The pleasure that coursed through her as his lips moved persuasively against hers was intoxicating, bringing forth passion and desires newly awakened.

His arms moved to encircle her and draw her against him, the length of his hard body against her softer one, the strength of his legs, his chest, the firm pressure of his arms as she relaxed and gave herself up to the pleasure of the moment.

If she could only think. She felt swept away with the euphoria spreading through her with Jared's caresses, the movement of his mouth on hers, seeking and finding a response.

When she pushed against him slightly he eased his hold, enabling her to move her arms, to reach around his neck and press her body up against his. Her fingers traced the strong muscles of his shoulders, the firm, warm column of his neck, threaded in the thick dark hair that brushed his collar.

The rhythmic warmth that pulsed at the center of her being warmed Kelsey, drove her to new desires, new heights of excitement, raised even further when Jared moved from her mouth to trail hot kisses across her cheek, down her throat, kissing the pulsating beat at its base.

"Don't wear this dress again unless it's for me alone," he said huskily.

"It's so pretty," she whispered, tasting him, her mouth along his jaw.

"I didn't like the way every man in the place stared at you."

She jerked back at that, staring up at him.

"I don't belong to you, Jared. You can't tell me what to do," she said, aware the longing that threatened to totally overwhelm her.

"Ah, but you do, my love. You belong to me as much as I belong to you. When are you going to admit it?"

"Never."

She jerked away. Turning, Kelsey fled for her room, slamming the door behind her, furious with herself. She'd let him get under her skin again! She knew he was trouble, that she would be the one hurt again if she let him near. She was drawn to him like a moth to flame. And she was the one who'd get burned.

Kelsey woke in the morning wondering why she was so depressed. For a long moment she lay on her side, watching the glimmer of sunshine peek in through the edges of the curtain.

Jared.

It always came back to Jared.

He'd tired of the ranch already. That explained why he'd invited guests. She refused to think he'd bring Pamela there for more, not with Aunt Ellie in residence.

There was so much work to do. They didn't have time for entertaining strangers. Of course, if the ranch wasn't ready for Grandma's before Jared left, it wouldn't matter. She'd planned to do it all alone to begin with.

But lately she'd come to rely on his help. And what of his plans to keep the cattle end of it going?

The guests weren't strangers to Jared. Pamela and he had starred in several movies together. He'd kissed her last night at the party. Who really knew how close they were?

And what was she, Kelsey, supposed to do when Pamela was there?

A smile lit her face.

Who did Jared expect to get the guest rooms ready? She'd cleaned hers and Aunt Ellie's. But Jared had to do his own.

And he'd darn well have to do the room for Pamela because Kelsey wouldn't lift a finger!

Her day brightened at the thought and at the knowledge that in only a few hours she'd be back home and able to put a safe distance between them.

She'd be so busy with the renovations and baking that she wouldn't have time to see him and his guests, wouldn't even have time to think.

Kelsey packed and thought of the previous evening. She'd enjoyed the preview showing of From the Ends of the Earth, Jared's film. Most of the party had been fun.

Suddenly she wondered how she was going to get through the rest of her life when he was gone?

Not knowing the answer to the last question, she was glad that her stay in Los Angeles was at an end.

The flight to Texas had been tense. Now it appeared

to be getting worse.

Jared was about to loss his temper.

Kelsey saw it flare and wondered how long it'd be before he exploded.

She smiled sweetly at him and turned away before she burst out laughing.

Things weren't going Jared's way and she was glad.

He always got things so easily, maybe it'd do him some good to be crossed now and then.

Pamela was the cause.

She'd arrived in the lobby of the hotel with enough luggage to fill the limo from the hotel. When they'd arrived in Dallas, it was too much, with what luggage each of the others had, to permit them all to ride in Kelsey's car together. Naturally Pamela had appropriated Jared and the car, leaving Kelsey and Jerry to ride together in a cab to her apartment.

The day only got worse. Pamela did nothing but complain. She was hot. The air was too humid. Kelsey's apartment was too stuffy. How could Jared bear to live in such a humid place? She had a headache from the reception last night. Traveling always upset her. How much further did they say it was to the cattle ranch?

But the real crux of the matter was the limitation Jared put on how much luggage Pamela was allowed to take to Windhaven. Unloading all of Pamela's bags at Kelsey's apartment, Jared told her one suitcase was all.

"How inhuman of you to expect me to choose only one!" Pamela cried dramatically "I need everything."

"No, you don't. We'll be riding, so bring jeans. It's hot and the house has no air conditioning, so bring some light clothes. Beyond that, you don't need four suitcases worth of clothes. You're only staying a few days. And we aren't having a party," he retorted.

Kelsey had her suitcase ready and leaned against the back wall of her living room, awaiting the outcome with bated breath. Would Jared prevail?

Pamela gave as good a hissy fit as any she'd seen but she could tell Jared was about to explode. How would his leading lady handle that?

She wondered if Pamela was always that temperamental.

Kelsey gazed around her apartment. She'd been here almost four years, but curiously it no longer felt like home. She was ready to get back to Windhaven to see how much had been done prepping the area for the new kitchen.

She'd been away too long, albeit only a few days. Grandma's needed her and she needed the fulfilling work.

Jerry picked up her suit case and suggested they wait for Jared and Pamela in the car.

He placed her suitcase into the trunk and went to sit in the back seat of the car, a thick adventure novel in his hand. Leaving the door open for some breeze, he was immediately engrossed in the book.

Kelsey wondered if this was old news to him. If he worked with Pamela before, he'd probably seen her temper tantrums.

Well, she was getting tired of waiting.

She went to the driver's side and opened the door, sounding the horn.

At the rate things were going Kelsey wondered if they'd even leave for Windhaven before dark. Pamela sure gave a good fight, but Kelsey also knew that Jared wasn't easy to shake once he'd made up his mind.

She sounded the horn again.

Jared came to the window and glared down at her.

"I'm leaving," she called up.

He held up one finger then disappeared from view.

Finally, Jared and Pamela came from the apartment, each carrying one small suitcase. Pamela was in a snit and refused to look at anyone. Which didn't stop her from regally appropriating the front seat. Jared gave her a hard look, which she didn't see and glanced wryly at Kelsey. He put their bags in the trunk and went to the driver's door.

"I'll drive," he said.

"Fine by me."

Trying not to laugh at his fate, Kelsey climbed into the back seat beside Jerry and opened her notebook—she had plans to finalize for the Markham account.

The drive to Windhaven seemed to drag in Kelsey's restless desire to get home quickly. The beauty of the hill country soon drew her attention, however, and she passed the time gazing out of the window. Ignoring Pamela's constant complaints and Jared's short answers, she let the serenity and beauty of the land soothe her.

As they drew near Windhaven, Kelsey's excitement rose. They turned on to the road that led home, past the cowboys compound, down the dusty road towards the house nestled in the tall old oak trees.

With a shock, she gazed at it.

It was lovely! The bright white paint gleamed in the afternoon sun and the shutters and trim were a deep, rich green. The front yard had been cut and watered, the grass already turning green.

It looked wonderful!

Her eyes blurred with tears as she saw the change. It was going to be perfect for Grandma's, exactly as she'd envisaged it.

She sought Jared's eye in the mirror. He was watching her, his eyes narrowed, his face expressionless.

"How?" she asked softly, blinking back the tears. She hadn't expected the trim to be painted already.

"Told Jim what I wanted. I'm sure Ellie had a hand in getting it all done in time. It's only the front, but makes a good first impression, huh?"

"It's perfect," she said softly, her smile happy, warm as she gazed at the old house. She'd plant flowers around the porch and hang lacy curtains in the front windows. It'd be the perfect setting for Grandma Mary's Cookies.

And home.

Ellie was sitting on the porch when they drew up and rose to greet them.

"Your rooms are all ready. Jared can help you with your bags," she said to the visitors once introductions were finished.

Kelsey turned to Jared, frowning. Did he get out of everything?

"Don't you think that was an imposition to ask Aunt Ellie to clean the rooms?" she hissed, turning away from Pamela and Jerry so that they wouldn't be embarrassed.

"I mentioned I was bringing guests and she offered— who am I to argue?"

He raised an eyebrow at Kelsey, giving a smug, satisfied smile at her frustration.

"I think I'll lie down, if it's okay with everyone. Staying up late last night and all the travel today has given me a headache," Pamela said dramatically as she mounted the shallow steps to the house. No mention of the fight in Dallas.

Jared carried Pamela's bags while Kelsey and Jerry were left to fend for themselves. Following a few moments later, Kelsey reached the top of the stairs in time to see Pamela standing in the doorway of the room across the hall, smiling up at Jared.

Kelsey's heart twisted when she saw them and she looked away.

"It's perfect. I'll see everyone at dinner."

Pamela closed the door with a definite click.

"Still miffed, is she?" Jerry asked, passing by Jared, glancing at the closed door to Pamela's room.

"Tired, I think. Ellie's put you in this room."

Jared opened the door to the room adjacent to Pamela's. Jared's smile had a teasing quality as he motioned to Jerry.

"Fine with me. If you have no plans for us for the rest of the afternoon, I'll take one of those chairs out front and sit beneath a tree and read my book. It's not often I have a quiet afternoon."

"Kelsey and I will be looking over what's been done around here, if you don't mind being on your own," Jared said as Kelsey slipped past and went to her room.

She closed the door and leaned back against it. How long were the guests staying? She ached with love for him—could she endure his involvement with Pamela under the same roof? She wished she had not gone to Los Angeles.

Slowly Kelsey changed into shorts and a cotton top. One thing was for sure—she refused to remain in her room all the time, much as she'd like to. In fact, she'd like to go to bed and not wake up until they'd all left.

Squaring her shoulders, however, she left to seek out Aunt Ellie and tell her the good news about Markham Enterprises.

Ellie was in the kitchen, working on a batch of cookies. Kelsey joined her and related all the news about the new account and reviewed exactly what she and Joseph Markham had discussed.

"It'll be a bit of a push until we get this place fully operational. What with you and me baking here. I need Suzanne and Muriel to keep the main business going in Dallas. That means we'll also have to package and drive to Willowby each day to ship. It's going to take a lot longer until the entire operation is here. Once we're in full operation we'll have a larger staff and be able to handle it easily, I think," Kelsey finished.

"It won't hurt us to work a little harder for a while. Have you seen the new kitchen foundation?" Ellie nodded through the window and Kelsey hurried over to look out.

" When will they start building the walls?"

It looked bigger than she'd thought it would.

"As soon as the foundation's deemed set up enough. That two by fours in the back are ready to go once the concrete's set. That contractor doesn't let any grass grow under his feet." Ellie liked hard workers. She had no time for malingerers.

"I want to see how big it feels from the inside. I'll be right back."

Kelsey dashed from the kitchen across the yard and to concrete slab. Stepping in where the front door would stand, she looked around. The ovens would go here. The stainless steel prep counters here and here. Looking up, she smiled at the view. She loved it!

"What are you doing?" Jared asked, coming to stand beside her.

He'd changed into shorts, a T-shirt and tennis shoes.

"I'm imagining what my new kitchen will look like."

"It's a concrete slab," he said.

She moved around him. "Here's where the sink will be. And here's for the ovens, the refrigerators and the alcove where the racks of cookies will cool. Then it leads into the packaging area and then shipping. He's graded the driveway to join up with the main drive so trucks can get in. It's going to be perfect."

She smiled at him, hoping he envisioned the building as it would be. As she saw it already.

He smiled at her joy and gave her a hug, drawing her against him. The warmth from his body spread to hers and Kelsey fought the wave of desire that spread through her. Jared grew more dangerous the longer he stayed.

She pushed gently against his chest, not unhappy when he wouldn't release her, but totally confused.

"Shouldn't you be with your guests?" she asked, staring at his mouth, afraid to meet his eyes.

Her body tingled from contact with his. Her heart pounded—could he tell?

Kelsey felt the strong beat of his heart beneath her

fingers, felt the strong muscles of his chest, and gave in to the longing to rub. The soft breeze through the shade trees caressed her cheeks, ruffled her tousled curls.

Being with Jared filled her with contentment.

She glanced up involuntarily. She was happy. She was happy being with him, having him hold her. If she only trusted him.

Without a word, he kissed her quickly, giving her a brief touch of heaven before pulling back and setting her away from him.

"We wouldn't want Pamela to get the wrong idea, would we?" Kelsey snapped out as he stepped back.

"And what would Pamela know or care about what we do?" He raised an eyebrow. "Are we jealous, Kelsey, love?" he asked sardonically, his smile hateful.

"Ha!" She turned away lest her flaming cheeks give her away.

Yes, she was jealous! She wanted him to pay attention to her, not some beautiful actress.

He scooped her up and Kelsey, startled, flung her arms around his neck for balance. Turning, Jared walked out into the yard.

"What are you doing? Put me down! What do you think—?"

"Shut up, Kelsey. I'm going to see Jim and you can come with me," he invited.

"You've done well over the last few years. I'm proud of you." His eyes were steady, sincere as he looked down at her.

The compliment was unexpected.

"Thank you. I worked hard, and was determined to

make it work. But Aunt Ellie helped."

She had to give credit where it was due.

"Maybe helped, but the success is because of you. This ranch is half yours. You need to come up to speed on all aspects, not just your bakery."

"I have to—"

Jared lowered her to her feet and drew her slowly to him again. This time his kiss was deeper, longer. She forgot everything—where she was, what she had been doing, what she should be telling this man. She floated on a cloud of happiness.

Kelsey wasn't sure her legs would support her much longer; they were giving way beneath her, delightfully weak with the languor his kiss caused. The blood pounded loudly in her ears heat rose in her to rival that of the hot Texas sun. And still it wasn't enough. But Kelsey didn't care at the moment for propriety; she only wanted to kiss Jared as long as time would permit.

The slamming of a door broke them apart. Kelsey was breathing heavily and was vaguely pleased to note that Jared was doing the same. At least she wasn't alone in the passion of the moment.

She licked her lips, tasted him, and her heart lurched in her breast. She couldn't tear her eyes from him and gazed at him.

"Come back to LA with me, Kelsey," Jared said urgently. "Give me a chance, love. Give us a chance again."

"You have nothing I want. My future is here. I've built a successful business which is now on the brink of expansion. I need to keep focused. I couldn't do that in LA."

She spun around and headed for the back door.

If only she hadn't come out this afternoon. Is only she hadn't kissed him back. Tears flooded her eyes. If she wanted to play the "if only" game, she'd do well to go back four years. If only she hadn't found that other woman at his place.

She heard the roar of the motorcycle and brushed the tears from her eyes and gazed sadly at spot of the new kitchen.

How was she to get through the next few weeks? Her heart was breaking again.

She wanted him to change, never to have cheated on their marriage, to be the wonderful cousin she'd worshiped as a child. He'd meant so much to her growing up. Always larger than life, exciting, smarter than she. She'd idolized him.

Maybe that was why finding he had feet of clay was so distressing. She'd thought her wonderful cousin perfect. And he wasn't.

She stood there for a long time, brushing the last traces of tears from her face. Taking a deep breath, she turned to enter the kitchen.

Kelsey kept busy for the remainder of the afternoon working with her aunt, baking and packaging cookies, and filling her in on the details she had for the Markham account.

Ten

Dinner was surprisingly enjoyable. Pamela and Jerry set out to charm everyone and even Kelsey laughed at their tales of hardships while filming and asked questions about the film industry.

Jared laughed and abetted them, avoiding Kelsey's eye, and ignoring her as much as good manners would allow.

She should have been happier, but she wasn't.

She was up early the next morning to size the wall in the living room in preparation for the papering. She wondered if Jared asked Billy or another of the cowboys to help her when it was time to paper. She'd be ready to start with this room tomorrow and the dining room as soon as she finished in here.

Jared joined her half an hour later.

"I thought you'd want to sleep in. Weren't you and your guests up late last night?" Kelsey asked, trying not to let the fact that he had excluded her last night bother her.

After the enjoyable dinner, Jared and his guests moved to the front porch. Kelsey helped her aunt clean up, then went to her room. She heard the soft murmur of conversation and the occasional laugh. She wished she'd joined them.

"I can work until they wake up."

He poured some of the sizing into another container and moved to a different wall.

They worked in silence.

He was upset about something. What? she wondered.

When Pamela and Jerry came downstairs, Jared went to join his guests. After they ate breakfast, Jared took them out to see the area he thought suitable for the movie. He was expecting others from the production to arrive the next day to determine if the landscape would be suitable, but he wanted Pamela and Jerry to see it first.

It set the pattern for the next few days. He showed off the ranch. Spent time with the production crew, introduced them to the cowboys. The day after they left, he took Pamela and Jerry into Dallas for the day. Pamela needed some of her things from the suitcases left behind in Kelsey's apartment.

Jared never invited Kelsey to join them. He worked each morning with her until the others were up, then took off.

He didn't ask anyone to help so Kelsey went to talk to Jim to get Billy's help. In three days they were finished. The rooms looked clean, fresh and ready for furniture.

Kelsey continued baking while the Hollywood crowd, as she called them, played. She tried not to be hurt they apparently had no interest in her joining them.

When the phone rang on the fourth day of their visit, Kelsey was at her desk, bringing her accounts up to date.

"Hello, is Jerry Longstreet or Pamela Hughes there?"

"They're staying here, but they're out right now."

"It's important that I reach them as soon as I can. Do you have any idea where they are?"

"In Dallas, I think. Do you have their cell numbers?"

"I do and I tried them both, but they keeps going to voice mail and I want to speak to them as soon as possible."

"I don't expect them back until late. I can have them call," Kelsey said, doodling on a pad by the phone. She crossed out the nonsense. It had been Jared's name.

"Ask them to call Mona."

Kelsey dutifully wrote it down and assured the caller she'd pass on the message.

She stared out of the window, envying the others their day in Dallas. Once again, she hadn't been invited.

Not that she'd have gone—there was too much to do here. But it would have been nice to be invited.

Looking at her calendar, Kelsey tried to calculate how much longer Jared would stay. When he left, could she convince him to sell her his share of Windhaven?

It was late when the others returned. Kelsey had already gone to bed, but wasn't asleep. She heard their laughter when they entered the house and a pang of loneliness hit.

Remembering the message, she drew on her robe and quietly descended the stairs.

Jared was pouring brandies for everyone when she entered the kitchen. The only room beside her office usable at this stage. It was pleasant with aroma from the day's baking still lingering.

All eyes swung to her. Pamela smiled happily, a

healthy glow of pink showing on her cheeks. Jerry was leaning contentedly against the counter, smiling too.

Jared glanced at her and turned back to his task, his lips tightening.

"You had a call today," Kelsey said to Pamela, and then nodded to Jerry. "Both of you, actually, from a Mona. She said it was important."

"Oh, my God, the children." Pamela went white."Where's my phone?"

"She said important, not urgent."

"We don't have cell service here," Jared said.

"Can I use your phone?" Jerry asked calmly, pushing away from the counter.

"Yes, this way."

Everyone hastened into the office, crowding the tiny room. Kelsey led the way to the desk and then went to leave, but Jared stood in the doorway and she didn't want to have to push past him. She watched as Jerry dialed and waited for the connection. Pamela stood beside him, almost pushing against him to get close to the phone. He reached his arm around her and pulled her even closer.

"Hello, Mona, it's Jerry."

His face was grave as he listened. Pamela never took her eyes from his.

"We'll be on the first plane out in the morning. You tell Pamela—she'll never believe me."

He thrust the receiver at her, his arm still around her.

Pamela talked for a few minutes then hung up.

"We shouldn't have come, should we? You wanted to go home, but I wanted to see Jared's ranch."

"It's okay. We'll be home in a few hours." Jerry

looked up at Jared and Kelsey. "Family emergency—kids came down with chickenpox, of all things. We'll have to book a flight out and leave as soon as we can."

"We'll leave right away for Dallas and you can get on the first flight out in the morning." Jared moved to the phone. "Kelsey can help you pack, Pamela."

Kelsey nodded and quietly led the way back upstairs. There was no need to wake Aunt Ellie, she thought. Time enough to tell her in the morning.

She was still surprised by the turn of events. Were Jerry's children the ones who were sick? Why was Pamela concerned?

She paused by Pamela's door and waited while Jerry gave the pretty actress a quick kiss. "It'll be fine. They will be fine, sweets. We'll be home in only a few hours. Go pack."

Pamela looked distraught and was grateful for Kelsey's help. With both of them folding and packing, it didn't take long.

"Thanks for having us, Kelsey," Pamela said, sitting on the edge of the bed. "I'm sure it was inconvenient with the renovation and all you're doing. But I always wanted to see an authentic cattle ranch. I think the production team was satisfied with the area Jared showed him. So we'll probably be back."

"I'm sure Jared was happy to have you here. And you were no trouble."

Only to my peace of mind, she added silently.

"No." Pamela smiled conspiratorially. "I think he regretted asking us the moment he'd done so. But I wanted to see it more than have good manners. Even Jerry gave in this time. He's really the best husband a woman could have."

Her eyes filled with tears.

"Husband?" Kelsey sank down on the edge of the bed in surprise.

"Jerry's your husband? I thought you and Jared..."

She snapped her mouth shut, her mind reviewing everything she knew about Pamela and Jerry. She remembered Jerry's fond talk about his girls. This was their mother?

Pamela laughed at that.

"What an impression you must have of me. In the first place, I wouldn't play around under my husband's nose. And Jared's not the type to play around at all. You're his cousin, you should know that."

"I don't know anything at all like that. I know that he does," Kelsey said stiffly, glad for pride's sake that Pamela didn't know she was more than Jared's younger cousin.

"Maybe he gives that impression. We all do in Hollywood. It adds something to the glamour of being a movie star. But Jared's different. Especially in Hollywood. He doesn't date, doesn't go to any party unless it's a command performance by the studio and he doesn't drink."

Kelsey looked down at her hands, twisting the belt of her robe. That picture didn't match what Kelsey had witnessed.

"I paid him a surprise visit in London once. He had a woman at his place then. She'd been there all night."

Her voice was low, and she tried hard to keep the pain from it.

Pamela went silent, staring at Kelsey, speculation rampant in her gaze.

"Are you the woman he loves, Kelsey?" Pamela asked gently.

Kelsey looked up.

"I've only known Jared a few years. Three, maybe. But we've become close, what with starring in two movies together and all. Once I teased him about not dating, and he told me he made a big mistake a while ago, let something come between him and the woman he loved. Now he doesn't date, doesn't drink, rarely parties, yet he brought you to the opening in LA. Are you that woman, Kelsey?" Pamela asked again, her expression sympathetic.

"I'm his wife," Kelsey said, her gaze holding Pamela's, the distress she felt whenever she thought of that morning in London evident in her eyes.

"Gracious the man's an idiot!" Pamela got up and walked impatiently around the room. She checked her bags, then looked out of the window at the dark night. Turning, she gazed at Kelsey.

"That explains why he's been so attentive to me this trip. He's trying to make you jealous. Did it work?"

Pamela tilted her head as she looked at Kelsey.

The loud knock on her door startled both women, then it was thrust open.

"Jared has a red-eye that leaves in a few hours. If we leave now, we'll be in Dallas in time to get the rest of your things from Kelsey's apartment and make the flight," Jerry said, glancing at the packed suitcase.

"I'm ready." Pamela smiled at Kelsey. "I think he really loves you," she said briefly, taking one of her bags and glancing dramatically around the room one last time.

Kelsey grabbed the other and followed.

She trailed them to the porch and exchanged farewells. She stopped Jared as he was ready to descend the stairs and offered him a key.

"What's that?" he asked suspiciously.

"A key to my flat, to get Pamela's bags. You can sleep there too after you get them to the airport. You've been up since early this morning. Don't drive home without sleep."

He looked at the key as if weighing the consequences of accepting it. Kelsey had lent it to him before when Pamela went to get things from her suitcase. It wasn't that big a deal.

"I'll stay at a hotel," he said, turning to descend the steps.

She slipped the key into his pocket. "Stay there. Why spend money if you don't have to?"

"There speaks a thrifty housewife," he said.

"Or someone who was poor for a while and had to make every dollar count."

He stiffened as he continued down the stairs, and Kelsey realized instantly she'd said the wrong thing.

Kelsey told her aunt the next morning about the reason for the abrupt departure of their guests—and the surprising situation she'd discovered.

"They were married," she said in wonder.

"I knew that," Ellie said, fixing her niece with a knowing look.

"I didn't know until last night."

"I wondered. But I thought you did know, I mean,

how did you not? You met them in LA, spent time around them. I'm sorry their children are sick."

"I thought she was flirting with Jared," Kelsey said slowly.

"And you were standing by and letting her? Where's your gumption, girl? Did you have that talk with Jared like I told you?"

"Sort of."

Ellie sniffed. "What kind of answer is that? Either you did or you didn't."

"Well, we started to, then—I wouldn't listen. Anyway, what could he say to change anything?"

He couldn't deny that the woman had been there.

"Well, if you want to be a coward all your life, so be it. I still advise sitting down with him and hashing everything out once and for all. You'd be no worse off than you are now. Even if there isn't a good explanation, maybe the man changed. He's crazy about you, anyone can see that."

"I'll be a lot worse off if we don't get these orders filled. I need to start advertising for more help. The kitchen will be ready before we know it, earlier than I'd hoped for."

"And won't I be glad? This kitchen is the focal point of any social gatherings here. Definitely not a way to run a business."

"We'll be all business as soon as all the renovations are finished. It'll be nice, won't it?" Kelsey's enthusiasm was waning. In fact it was hard to get enthusiastic about anything anymore. All she thought about was Jared.

"The tearoom will be charming. We'll increase our

sales by drop-in customers for the tearoom and be able to handle the expansion the Markham account will bring with the new kitchen—as long as we get enough help. Who knows what new accounts we can get in the next few years. I'm excited."

Kelsey nodded absently. Her thoughts were on Jared. Again.

"Kelsey, you're wool-gathering, did you hear me!" Ellie's voice broke into her reverie.

She blinked and looked at her aunt in surprise. It was getting worse. What was she to do about it?

Jared didn't return that day, nor the next. Kelsey wondered if he'd returned to LA with his friends and left her to finish the renovations by herself.

She vacillated between being annoyed that he hadn't said goodbye, that he hadn't seen the project through, and relief that she didn't have to be around him.

On the second day, Ellie mentioned at tea that Jared called and would return to Windhaven the next day.

"He asked if we needed anything from Dallas and I gave him a list. He's picking up some of the shipping boxes we use. We're running low."

"Did he mention why he was still there?" Kelsey asked, relieved to learn that he was coming back.

"No."

Ellie had a satisfied air about her as she sipped her tea. Kelsey curiosity rose. Ellie would surely tell her if it was anything she needed to know.

The living room was finished except for furnishings. The lace curtains she'd bought were perfect. All that was left at that point was to get tea tables and chairs.

She thought briefly of the furniture her parents stored in their attic. A couple of pieces would be perfect for that old-fashioned vibe.

Maybe she'd go home for a visit. It'd been four years since she'd been home. Telephone calls and Skype had helped bridge the gap. Now she was suddenly homesick for her family.

They were pleased about her success, she knew from emails and conversations with her mom.

When all the renovations were complete, she'd invite them for the grand opening.

She missed her mother, Aunt Lilith, and her sister Corey.

With the success of Grandma's behind her, maybe she could put up with all their I-told-you-so comments about her marriage.

Kelsey stood in the middle of the living-room the next afternoon and slowly turned around, taking in the clean windows, the lacy white curtains that framed the view of the distant hills. The fresh wallpaper gave the room its hint of old-fashioned times. The floor was cleaned and polished and the trim was spotless. It came out precisely as she'd envisaged it.

"Want to take a break?" Kelsey asked Ellie when she wandered into the kitchen and headed for the fridge for some lemonade. It was a warm day and it'd be nice to sit on the front porch and relax.

"Sure. This last batch won't be cooled enough to box for a little while."

Ellie took two glasses from the cabinet and followed her niece to the porch.

The house blocked the afternoon sun, the overhanging limbs of the shade trees shading the rest of the porch. It was cooler than the hot kitchen. Sipping her drink, Kelsey relaxed and let her eyes roam over the ranch.

"Jared insists we keep the cattle aspect going," she said again, remembering his earlier plans for the ranch.

"And does he plan to stay on and run that side of things?" Ellie asked sharply.

"No. He begins filming for the next picture soon. His boss at Tri-Color said at the opening that they had to meet at the end of the month, so I guess he'll be gone by then."

"I don't think you can run the ranch and Grandma's at the same time," Ellie said, a worried furrow on her brow.

"I can't. I wouldn't even want to try—there's too much to learn about cattle. I'll stick to baking."

Kelsey gazed down the road. Was that a car turning in? Her car?

Her heart sped up slightly while she tried to remain calm. It was her car. Jared was almost home.

He drew to a stop beneath the trees and killed the engine. For a long moment he remained in the car and Kelsey wondered what he was doing. She couldn't see him because of the sun's glare on the windshield.

He got out and joined them on the porch.

"Did they make their flight in time?" Kelsey asked.

"No problem."

He looked tired.

"Want some lemonade?" Ellie asked as he sank down on one of the chairs.

At his nod, Kelsey stood abruptly. "I'll get a glass."

The words Pamela had spoken that last night echoed in her head. She'd kept them at bay until now. But, seeing him again, she was reminded of what Pamela had said.

That Jared had said he'd made a mistake, never socialized, was cutting himself off from family and friends, not enjoying himself when he wasn't working— his idea of penance?

Kelsey knew she needed to talk to Jared, to find out all he cared to tell her and go on. The suspicions and imaginings couldn't be any worse than the real thing. She'd been too young, too immature at the time to deal with things.

She hoped she'd grown up a bit since then.

Once she knew, she'd deal with it and put it all behind her.

Kelsey returned to the porch and poured a glass of lemonade for Jared. Sitting near Ellie she smiled brightly.

"What did you do in Dallas?"

He'd been gone for three days. How long did it take to deliver someone to the airport?

His eyes narrowed and he studied her for a long moment before responding.

"If you want nothing from me, Kelsey, why would you want information on what I did with my time?" he said scornfully.

Kelsey blinked at that, feeling as if he'd slapped her, stunned at his answer. Her eyes darkened at the insult and she turned away, lest he see the pain he'd inflicted.

"I asked a civil question. You needn't answer if you don't wish."

"I got roaring drunk and laid every woman I got my

hands on. Isn't that what you expected?" he said, his voice hard, bitter.

"Jared!" Ellie's voice was shocked.

"Maybe you'd better go start dinner, Aunt Ellie. This is between Kelsey and me." Jared's gaze never left Kelsey's face.

Ellie hesitated a moment, then nodded. With a quick glance at Kelsey's stricken face, she entered the house, the screen door closing quietly behind her.

"A simple 'none of your business' would be as effective," Kelsey said in a low voice, anger starting to build within her. Was he mocking her?

"I went to see a lawyer. If you want a divorce, I'll give you one. We can finish the proceedings now and I'll send whatever else is needed from Los Angeles."

Kelsey's eyes sought his, locked with his gaze. Her throat. Her heart stopped, she was sure of it. Black clouds tinged the edge of her vision, and she wondered if time would stop and she could just die.

Jared's dark eyes were hard as they gazed back down at Kelsey. His mouth was a tight line, his face as hard as if carved from granite. He stared at her and said nothing.

When her stomach began to roll, she was afraid she'd be sick. She wasn't ready for any of this. She wasn't up to anything right now.

With shaky legs, she rose and moved towards the house, feeling as if she was in a dream, or a nightmare. As she reached the door, Jared stopped her. In his hand was the key to her flat.

"I stayed there after all," he said, reaching down to pull her hand up, wrapping her fingers around the key. His touch burned yet it was the only warmth Kelsey felt. She was cold. As cold as the reality of their relationship.

She turned and went into the house, climbed the stairs to her room. As she collapsed on to her bed she heard the mighty roar of the motorcycle, its noise fading as Jared rode away from the house, away from her and the mockery their marriage had been.

It was over, then.

Finally.

Why she should be surprised, shocked or hurt was beyond her.

She'd thought they were already divorced. What had been a surprise was when Jared had told her they weren't.

Kelsey stared at the ceiling, too drained even for tears. She wondered if she'd ever have enough energy to move. It was strange; she'd been at odds with Jared since he arrived. Conversely, she'd felt more alive than at any time in the last four years.

Memories of early years flooded. The times his family had visited hers. The times when as a child she'd seen her adored cousin from East Texas. The last visit when he'd asked her to marry him. How could one person be so happy she'd wondered.

Only to end up like this.

She passed up dinner when Ellie called.

Changing into a soft white cotton gown when it got dark, she crawled back into bed and lay there, trying not to remember, trying to plan for the future.

Instead her thoughts focused on Jared.

Ellie was right. She needed to know exactly what had

happened, to see if it'd put things in their proper perspective.

If he left now, would she ever see him again?

Would Jared come home tonight? Could she ask him tonight, find out once and for all and see where it led her?

Ellie was right as she often was. She was a coward.

She slipped from her bed and stole down the hall. The house was in darkness. It was late, already after midnight. Ellie slept. Jared wasn't home. Wasn't coming home? Kelsey didn't know.

She opened the door to his room, immediately smelling his scent, the scent that reminded her of the open air and hot sun and Jared. Closing the door behind her, she leaned against it. He wasn't here, but she almost felt his presence.

Smiling at her notions, she drifted to the window and stared out over the moonlit land. Jared's room was on the side of the house. She gazed at the dark shadows the trees threw over the yard, shading the new kitchen in the moonlight as they would shade it in the sunlight. The hills in the distance were only a dark silhouette against the moonlit sky.

She stared from the window for a seemingly endless time, remembering her cousin's visits and her family and all the plans she'd made as a girl.

Then she heard the bike. It was muffled, as always when he came in late. His thoughtfulness struck her again.

She turned to face the door, her eyes accustomed to the darkness, her heart beating faster and faster.

Eleven

In only seconds Kelsey heard his tread on the steps, slow, tired. When he opened the door, she felt a hint of uncertainty. What if he threw her out without talking to her? What if he was still angry with her? What if what he had to say shattered any semblance of control?

Jared closed the door and slumped against it, sighing softly. Kelsey's heart ached at the sight. She always thought of him as strong, fearless.

Now he looked... defeated.

"Jared," she said softly.

His head snapped up and he saw her outlined against the window.

"What are you doing here?"

He pushed away from the wall and stalked over to her.

Kelsey stood her ground. He looked predatory in the darkness, all trace of defeat gone.

"I wanted to talk to you," she said breathlessly.

"About what?" He was only inches from her and anger emanated from him in waves. "Do you want to know where I was tonight? Is that it? Because we share this inheritance it doesn't give you the right to know everything about my life. Remember? You want nothing from me."

Had that hurt him? He kept repeating that—had her statement bothered him in some deep way?

Before Kelsey said anything, however, Jared turned away and flung himself down on his bed, propping himself up against the headboard with the pillows.

"Not that it's any of your business, but I went first to see Jim about the ranch, then went into town, to the bar. I spent the night playing darts and imagined the target was your cold, unforgiving heart every time!"

Kelsey jumped at the bitterness in his tone. Slowly she moved away from the window towards the bed, as if drawn by invisible threads. Sinking down gingerly at the foot of the bed, she looked at him, wishing she could see him better, but not wanting the intrusion of light.

"Jared, tell me what happened that morning I came to London."

"What's there to tell? You know it all. You've always told me that."

His voice was flat, dead.

"I'm sorry. I was wrong. Please tell me what happened," she said gently, her eyes fixed on his.

She saw them gleaming in the moonlight, knew he was watching her.

"What difference does it make now? I left it too long," he said.

"Please tell me how it happened," she whispered. She needed to know exactly what had happened so that she might go on with her life.

Jared sat up and reached for her, drawing her up

against him, resting her against his chest as he settled back against the headboard. Kelsey resisted for a moment, held herself stiffly, then gradually relaxed against him. Her legs rested beside his, her arm loosely encircled his waist and her head rested on his chest. She heard the strong, steady beat of his heart. He tucked her head beneath his chin and was silent, holding her, not moving, not speaking.

Finally he began, and Kelsey closed her eyes, afraid to hear what he'd say.

"Where do I begin? It's like a lifetime ago."

For Kelsey it seemed as clear as yesterday.

"I missed you. We'd been separated for so many months."

His voice was low, soft in the nighttime darkness.

"So it's my fault?" she said softly, a frown between her brows.

"No, actually there is no fault, except perhaps lack of trust and stubborn pride. I was caught up in the excitement of the filming, the glamour of it all. Being in London's totally different from Texas. And I was young and brash and cocky. I thought I had the world by the tail."

Kelsey knew that. He'd always been bolder than most men. Even other brash Texans. And the adulation he'd received from his growing fame in films added to it.

"It was heady, frankly. I loved it. The studio promoted me, building the star image. Every tabloid in the country had my picture on its cover at one time or another, always with a different woman. Most of them I didn't even know, just paused beside them at a party, or opening, or something. A flash and the camera captured me and my latest." He chuckled mirthlessly. "My latest insinuation only."

Kelsey was glad she hadn't seen those tabloids.

"You know the filming went on longer than anyone thought it would that time. We had overruns, delays, retakes like I'd never seen before or since. It was a costly film and tempers were getting short towards the end."

His hand threaded itself through her hair, holding her against him. He breathed in the soft, sweet scent of her, hating to have to continue.

"Mmm?" she said to show that she was listening.

"Finally it was over. And we had a huge cast party to celebrate London's portion being in the can. Everyone was in high spirits. Champagne flowed. It was the wildest party I'd ever been to. Everyone hugging everyone else, kissing. And I was missing you. I hadn't seen you in months. Even your emails had tapered off. And you remember how hard it was to connect by phone with our schedules and the time difference."

Kelsey listened to his heart as it beat steadily. One hand caressed her hair, the other rubbed her back in lazy circles designed to relax her.

"Sally Masters was a young starlet who had a small part in the film. She hung on me all night. Mostly because I was the star, I think. But I didn't notice. I was too busy getting roaring drunk. Everyone was so happy the location part was finally over. Everyone had someone to share that happiness with, except me. So I drank to forget that you were six thousand miles away and I was all alone."

He was quiet for a moment, as if remembering the party, how apart he'd felt from the others, how he had missed Kelsey, longed for her to be with him.

"The next thing I knew, I woke up in bed with the world's worst hangover, and you and Sally staring down at me. Then you turned away and stormed out without even talking to me or listening to me."

Kelsey's mind flashed back to that morning. The heat of the day not yet started, it had been cool and pleasant as she'd waited excitedly for her husband to open the door. How stunned she'd been when Sally had greeted her, especially scantily dressed as she'd been.

She remembered his shocked look when they'd wakened him, remembered the words Sally had said.

"She said you slept together."

"She lied," he said evenly. His heart did not change pace. Kelsey could hear its steady beat beneath her ear.

Had she been wrong all this time? Had Jared let her believe what he knew to be wrong all these years?

"After I left, then what?"

"First I forced the story out of Sally. She'd brought me home knowing I'd had too much to drink. Planning a seduction scene in the morning, she'd slept in one of the spare rooms. She'd been a troublemaker from the first. When you arrived, she made the most mischief she could, hoping, I guess, that I'd go for her if you left."

"Then you really didn't sleep with her?" Kelsey exclaimed. Why hadn't he told her this before?

"Not only did I not sleep with her, I didn't even know she was in the house until I woke up that morning. And I got rid of her pretty quick after you left."

Kelsey squeezed her eyes shut, blood pounding in her head as the words made their impact.

"Then why not tell me? Why have you been gone for four years?"

Dare she believe what he was saying now?

"I tried to find you. I called the airlines, called every hotel in the area. I guess you never checked in anywhere."

"No, I went right back to the airport and got on the next flight out. It was leaving for Calgary. I stayed overnight there, then flew to Dallas and Aunt Ellie."

"Then I got mad, so frigging mad I could hardly see straight. How dare you think that about me? I asked myself that question a million times. If that was what you thought of me, of my morals, of my wedding vows, the heck with you. I didn't need you."

Kelsey knew about his temper and how stubborn he could be.

But four years?

She felt the tears began to flow. Her heart ached so. She should have given him a chance to explain that morning. She should have stood her ground and not run.

But she'd been stunned. Too stunned to think straight.

If he loved her, if he still wanted her why did he wait so long before coming. Why not tell her the first day?

She knew why. She never gave him the chance.

Tears spilled down her cheeks, soaking into his shirt. What was she going to do? What did Jared want to do?

"Oh, don't cry. Don't cry, baby. I'm a stupid idiot with a fierce temper. But I didn't mean to cause you such grief. I finally calmed down enough to send you an email, but you never replied, never contacted me, never gave me a chance to explain."

"I didn't get an email. Nothing from you all this time."

Had it gone astray, into spam, lost in the ether?

"Why did you let me go on thinking what I did?"

"I never meant for it to go on for so long. But you weren't the only one hurt. For heaven's sake, Kelsey, you've known me since we were kids. How could you ever think I'd cheat on you?"

She shook her head, but didn't have a word in her defense.

"I was angry and hurt. I thought I'd let you cool off and then we'd get together, talk things through. But the days slipped by. It was ages before I was over being so angry. Especially when you didn't write back. When you didn't seem to care about me. I wanted your trust. How could you think that of me if you loved me?"

"But I saw—and she said....." Her tears wouldn't stop.

He held her tighter, moving his arm slowly up and down her back until Kelsey grew calmer.

"Then I got the letter from the attorney about the divorce. That upped my anger even more. So I didn't sign, didn't do anything with it. When I learned of Uncle Henry's legacy followed by your formal letter offering to buy me out, I got mad all over again and decided enough was enough."

Slipping down on the mattress, Jared pulled her completely on top of. He bent his mouth to hers and she met him, tears still wet on her cheeks.

His kiss was sweet and gentle—an apology for all the hurt and anger and misunderstanding.

His hands roamed over her back, no longer soothing but inflaming. When he touched the edge of her nightgown, he moved it up a few inches, feeling the smooth silk of her leg.

Kelsey jerked back, her eyes wide as she tried to see him in the dim light.

So it'd been her own lack of trust and his pride that had kept them apart for four years.

She needed to think. She couldn't with him touching her.

She scooted away from him, stood up, almost falling as she stumbled back, away from the tempting bed, dashing the tears from her cheeks.

"Kelsey, I want you."

"No." She refused to be swayed by sweet lips and passion. She needed to think. Was everything he said true?

How could he have let her go on for four years believing he'd had an affair. How could she not have pressed for the truth before now.

"You came to my room, I didn't go to yours."

"I only wanted an explanation," she protested as she watched him with wary eyes.

"I'm not innocent in all this. I let my own pride keep me away. But another thing I thought about when I heard about Uncle Henry was the fact he never married. Never had children of his own to leave this ranch to. Only a distant nephew and niece. Life's short, I let my pride keep me away from you for four years. I kept hoping you'd write back. I can't tell you the hope that rose when I saw your name on the envelope, only to be dashed when you offered to buy out my half of the ranch."

He sat on the edge of the bed and ran his fingers through his hair.

"I've wanted you back since that morning. LA was was only a taste of what was and what can be again. Don't leave tonight."

He said he'd written. Kelsey wished fervently that she'd received it. Would it have changed things?

"What's it to be, Kelsey?"

She met his eyes. "Maybe—maybe I don't want a divorce," she said breathlessly.

Jared stared at her for endless moments. "Maybe? Don't you know?"

She loved him. She always had.

How could either one of them have let themselves remain apart for four?

He hadn't said he loved her.

"Jared, I don't know what to do," she whispered, her eyes distressed.

"Then say after me, Jared, I love you, I want to stay your wife. I want to be with you."

"Jared, I love you. Do you love me?"

All the hurt and anguish of the past four years came out in her voice.

"Good grief, Kelsey, how can you even ask?"

He rose and crossed over to her, pulling her against him in a warm hug, resting his head on her soft curls. "You're a part of me. My life's incomplete without you. These last years have been hell. I ached for you. I'm so sorry."

"But you never say you love me." Her voice was still a whisper.

"I do love you, Kelsey, more than life. I don't know—maybe it's because I've been acting so long, saying words that others write, that I have a hard time telling you that. But that doesn't mean I don't. I tried to show you in everything I ever did. I've loved you since you were a teenager, playing romantic heroines with your sister. I only hoped you'd stay single long enough to grow up and let me marry you! If you want the words, I'll say them every day. I love you, Kelsey Martin, now and forever."

"How would you like it if I never said I loved you?" she asked, pressing against his chest, trying to become one with him.

He was silent for a long moment. "Point taken. I love you."

"I love you. Oh, Jared, I love you so much. I never want us to be parted again. Never!"

"Then we won't be. You can come with me when I'm filming and Aunt Ellie can keep Grandma's going. Between films we'll come here and watch the ranch grow and your business. But always together. And it looks like the next film will be right here in Texas."

"It's a done deal?"

"Good as. I haven't heard anything to change that. But I have until the end of the month before I have to report. We can have an extended honeymoon before filming begins."

"I think life with you will be one long honeymoon," she. "One... long... glorious..." she said between kisses.

"Honeymoon. I love you, Kelsey," he finished impatiently, stopping her words for a long time.

If you liked **Movie Star Cowboy**,
you may enjoy **Rebel Heart** from
The Harts of Texas series

If you enjoyed **Movie Star Cowboy**
please consider leaving a review.

More Books by Barbara McMahon

Cowboy Hero Series
The Cowboy Next Door
Cowboy's Bride
One Stubborn Cowboy
Crazy About a Cowboy
Never Doubt a Cowboy
Cowboy Marshal
Summer Cowboy
Second Chance Cowboy
Movie Star Cowboy

Cowboys of Wildcat Creek
Valentine's Cowboy Rescue
Shelly and the Cowboy
Kristi's Cowboy Hero
Holly's Reluctant Cowboy
A Cowboy for Eliza

Sweet Reunion Romance Collection
Unexpected Reunion
Unpredictable Reunion
Unanticipated Reunion

The Harts of Texas Series
Rebel Heart
Tangled Hearts
Reckless Heart

Ultimate Billionaires Series
The Cynical Sheikh
Falling for the Sheikh
A Sheikh of Her Own
The Unforgettable Sheikh

Rocky Point Series
Rocky Point Legacy
Rocky Point Reunion
Rocky Point Promise
Rocky Point Hero
Rocky Point Inn
Rocky Point Dawn

The Talmadge Sisters Series
Letters to Caroline
Michelle's Marriage Deal
Trusting Abby

Tropical Escapes Series
Island Rendezvous
Come into the Sun
Island Paradise

A Sweet Clean Christmas Romance Collection
The Christmas Cop
The Cowboy's Special Christmas
A Soldier's Christmas
A Teaspoon of Mistletoe
The Christmas Locket
A Key West Christmas

Sweet Romance Stand-alone Collection
Because of You
Cowboy Charade
I'll Take Forever
Jared's Promise
Mail Order Bride
Not Really Married
Sweet Meant To Be
The Cowboy Comes Home
The Paper Marriage
Trusting Jake
The Banished Bride